ADDICTED TO YOU

ERIN O'REILLY

Also by Erin O'Reilly

Next Time
Ready for Love
Return to Me
If I Were a Boy
Through the Darkness
Deception
Fearless
'55 Ford
Fractured
That Kiss
Revelations
Wolf at the Door
Sandcastles
Spectre of Fear

When Hell Meets Heaven Series
Echoes of the Past
Paradox of Love
The End Game
Requiem

With JM Dragon
Say You Won't Go
Against All Odds
Take Me as I am
Echoes of the Past
The End Game
Requiem
Earthbound
New Beginnings
Atonement

ADDICTED TO YOU

ERIN O'REILLY

Affinity
Rainbow Publications

2019

Addicted to You
© 2019 by Erin O'Reilly

Affinity E-Book Press NZ LTD
Canterbury, New Zealand

1st Edition

ISBN: 978-1-98-858805-6

Editor: Angela Koenig
Proof Editor: Alexis Smith
Cover Design: Irish Dragon Design
Production Design: Affinity Publication Services

ACKNOWLEDGMENTS

I began writing this story many years ago and as it is with most things time forgot where I was going with this story. Add to that chemicals for lung carcinoids and my mind was more than jumbled when I took this story out to continue writing. With that in mind I have been fortunate for those who were watching my back to keep *Addicted to You* on track.

If it hadn't been for my friend, Julie, 'Addicted to You' wouldn't have seen the light of day. I constantly asked her questions about the story line and she was always available and ready to help me. Once the story was finished, Affinity's outstanding beta editor and my friend, Nancy pointed out places that needed tightening up and those that made her think "what the hell does she mean by that?" As always, Angela did a fantastic job of editing my story pointing out where I did or didn't have those troublesome commas and other punctuation nightmares. Next in this journey of 'Addicted to You' Alexis gave the manuscript a critical eye for all those pesky typos that always seem to come out of nowhere. Lastly is Alice who helps me out by formatting the completed story into eBooks. To all of you dear, wonderful ladies, thank you for watching my back when my brain was coming up empty.

DEDICATION

For Julie and Nancy who always have my back even when my brain is scattered.

TABLE OF CONTENTS

PROLOGUE

The early afternoon was cold and gray with the sun occasionally peeking out, promising warmth that it never gave. After having lunch nearby, Elin Prescot leaned against the wall of the Empire State Building viewing deck and looked at the vast expanse of the city. When life threw her a curve ball and she needed grounding, she always came to this place. Something about the immensity of it all made her realize just how insignificant her woes were. But, for some reason, Elin just couldn't get her head around what she was now considering. She had a wonderful life and her career had just taken a new and exciting turn. Yet, here she was, considering throwing it all away for something that experience told her would never work out. Elin unconsciously rubbed her arm while recalling every detail

1

from the moment she first met Marissa Banks. After all these years and despite all that had happened, she could still feel the tug of the woman, and released a growl.

"How did I get here? How did I let this happen?" Elin wrapped her arms around her body looking for warmth but found none.

CHAPTER ONE

Elin stood at the front window in her apartment, with her arms folded, watching rain and recalling the day she started toward her dream life…

"Mommy, she needs more clothes."

"Sweetheart, I don't have the money for that."

"But, Mommy, she only has two outfits. How can I play with her without clothes?"

"Tell you what we can do." Dorothy Prescot knelt and took the doll from her daughter's hands. "I can show you how to make clothes for her." She smiled. "That's what granny did for me."

"Really?" Elin's eyes opened wide and she clapped her hands before jumping up and down. "Oh, Mommy, can we do it now?

From that moment on Elin began designing clothes. She had the best-dressed dolls around and all her friends continually begged her to make outfits for their dolls too.

Thirteen years later, after all the self-teaching and mentoring by her mother, her dreams finally came true. She could still see the look on her mother's face the day the mail came...

"Mom, Mom, look at this!" Elin came flying into the kitchen.

Her mother took the official looking paper and read it before smiling broadly. "I'm so proud of you, darling." Dorothy wrapped her daughter in a warm hug.

"Thanks, Mom. Can you believe that it is really happening? Parsons accepted me, and once I graduate from there anything is possible." She grinned. "I just know it."

†

Five years later, Elin graduated from Parsons School of Design at the top of her class with a bachelor's and master's degree. Her dream was on its way to fulfillment when she accepted an apprenticeship at the upscale Boutique La René that specialized in all types of apparel for women in business. The shop, situated in the fashion district of New York City, had a long, impressive list of clients that included executives, politicians, stockbrokers, and many renowned businesswomen from around the country. She had spent the last six months learning the business from the boutique's owner, Bess Matthews.

"Good morning, Elin, did you have a pleasant weekend?" Bess asked when Elin walked into the store.

"The usual—cleaning, washing clothes, and shopping for groceries." Elin smiled. "How about yours?"

"I spent it with my daughter and her family." Bess shook her head and then laughed. "I'm getting too old to chase a three-year-old around."

"When I go to my cousin's house and watch her kids run around, I always wonder where they get all that energy. I think their mother tunes it all out because it never seems to faze her."

"My daughter is the same way. Well, the day has come, you are no longer an intern. We have a new client coming in and I want her to be your client. I know you will do a fantastic job with her, Elin." Bess clapped her hands, then picked up a folder and held it out. "This is her information and,"—she looked at her wristwatch—"you have three hours to familiarize yourself with her."

"Um. Thank you. Wow, what a way to start the week." Elin could feel excitement bubbling but there also was a modicum of fear. This had the potential of making or breaking her. She could feel Bess's chestnut brown eyes appraising her and, for a fleeting moment, she wondered if Bess was regretting the decision.

"It certainly is. I remember my first client and how the owner at that time had to come to my rescue." Bess had a bemused look on her face before she patted Elin's arm. "There is nothing to worry about, you'll do fine. I've watched you work and, of all the interns I've had over the years, you are by far the most promising."

"I won't let you down and you won't be sorry for trusting me."

"There is no doubt in my mind that you will do wonderfully." She handed the folder with Marissa Banks's name on it. "Here is the information I obtained from Ms. Banks's phone interview and the information she sent me. Are you clear on how to handle everything?"

"Yes. First, we will have a friendly conversation over coffee so I can get to know about her life, her job, and her clothing preferences. Then I will make an additional appointment to show her what I would suggest she wear." Elin thought for a moment. "Do you want to sit in?"

"No, my dear, I am sure you will do wonderfully." Bess smiled fondly and patted her shoulder.

†

Elin picked her favorite consultation room and went inside. The room was decorated with antiques and had a warm, comfortably friendly atmosphere. She sat in a chair that was at a highly polished square table and laid the folder in the middle. Elin ran a finger across the name and smiled while a thrill of excitement coursed down her spine. *Marissa Banks, my very first customer.* With that thought firmly in her mind she opened the folder and saw an eight by ten of a woman with black hair standing beside a desk with her arms akimbo and her ankles crossed. She had on a designer pencil suit with a red silk blouse and a string of black pearls around her neck. Elin had to catch her breath. In a word, her new client was stunning. There was a raw power exuding from her and Elin began worrying that she would never sell Marissa Banks anything.

On the next page, Elin learned that Marissa was forty-three-years old, and held masters degrees in both finance and business. Her eyes tracked down the page to see the woman's occupation and she frowned. What the hell was a venture capital firm? She'd better look that one up. The last thing she wanted was to look ignorant during the initial interview. She shook her head as she noted her new client's height, five foot nine, and weight, one hundred and fifty-two pounds. She flipped back to the photograph. If she had to guess, Elin would say she weighed less than that.

After turning on her laptop, Elin did a search to find that venture capital firms invested in startup companies. They pooled funds to invest in businesses that they thought would provide investors with high rates of return. For a moment, she puzzled over what it all meant and then decided to delve into the job description more. She learned her new client was a senior partner of the venture capital firm Rosen, Blake, Banks and Schiefer, and her salary was in the millions.

"I wonder if Bess knew?" Elin tapped a pen against the prepared document before she stood and left the room.

†

"Bess, do you have a moment?"

"I can tell by your frown that there's a problem. What is it?"

"Do you know anything else about Marissa Banks?"

"I'm not following you. I checked her file and from what I could see everything was there. Is something missing?" Bess had a perplexed look on her face.

"Well," Elin blew out a breath, "I've looked into her job and I think she is the kind of person who would eat me for an appetizer then spit me out."

"Why do you say that? I vet all of our clients and there were no red flags with the woman." A reassuring smile came to Bess' face. "I think you have the first client jitters." She patted Elin's arm. "Trust me, you'll do fine. I remember my first client and—"

Elin's eyes then darted around the reception area. "Where's Camille? Who is going to greet my client?"

"Breathe, Elin. Camille's mother took a tumble and they took her to the hospital."

"Oh, no. Is her mother okay? What about Ms. Banks? Should I just stand here and wait for her?"

"Elin, you need to calm down…everything is going to be fine." Bess patted Elin's shoulder. "I am going to do Camille's job today so there are no worries."

"Okay." Elin blew out a long breath. "Right. First client jitters. I've got it under control."

Just then the bell over the door jingled as a tall, well-dressed woman walked in. Elin felt another surge of panic and it wasn't the excitement that one feels when starting down a new road. The lady oozed power and something else. Danger.

She gulped in a breath. "I can do this," she told Bess and walked briskly toward the client with her hand outstretched.

"Ms. Banks? I'm Elin Prescot and I will be helping you today." She held out her hand.

"I understood that I'd be working with Ms. Matthews and not some underling. Isn't she here?"

"Bess Matthews is the owner and she has assigned me to advise you." Elin took a deep breath and lowered her hand, a look of anger and irritation crossed her face. Elin trembled as she gave the woman a discrete once over. "If you object, I can get her for you."

"Ms. Matthews came highly recommended, and frankly I know nothing about you."

Elin shivered. Marissa Banks's eyes seemed to be sizing her up much as Elin guessed she would a business proposal. *There's no way I'm letting her intimidate or bully me into giving up.*

"I understand. Listen, I'll make a deal with you." Elin's stomach, which seemed to be erupting in waves of nausea, belied her outward confidence.

"I'm listening," came the growled response.

"We can go into the consultation room and have a conversation about my credentials and what your expectations are." Elin searched the eyes that were a darker blue than hers and saw no objection. "If at any time you feel that you would prefer that Ms. Matthews be your consultant, I will happily get her for you."

"I don't deal with underlings, but since I am already here, I will give it a try." She sighed, deeply clenching her jaw.

†

I don't need this shit. Marissa surveyed the shop girl's body, then she squeezed her thighs tightly as a wave of pleasure surged through her body. *I can do with some eye-candy for a bit before I dismiss her for her boss to take over.*

"Please, take a seat, Ms. Banks. Can I interest you in something to drink?"

"Coffee, black would be good." Marissa sank down in the overstuffed chair surprised at its comfort. She had spied two Spode cups, a plate of crackers, brie, and fruit, and her stomach grumbled, reminding her that she hadn't eaten yet.

Elin filled one of the cups with coffee, placed it in front of her, and gestured toward the plate. "Please help yourself."

Once settled, Marissa listened as the young girl began her interview and looked at her watch. *I'll give her five minutes and then demand someone else.*

"May I call you Marissa?"

"That will be fine."

"Thank you. I know you answered a lot of questions when you made the appointment, but if you don't mind, I would like to ask them again."

"Why? Didn't you read what I told Ms. Matthews?" Marissa fixed the young girl with a look of annoyance and all thoughts of toying with the shop girl vanished. *This girl doesn't know a damn thing. God, what have I gotten myself into? Incompetence is unacceptable.*

"I didn't read the document, Ms. Banks, because I wanted to have an impression of you that is not tainted by previous knowledge." Elin straightened her shoulders. "I graduated the top of my class from Parson's with a degree in fashion design and then an MBA. I have interned with Alan Steven and just finished another internship at this shop, and I'm now a full time consultant at Boutique La René."

"Frankly, that means nothing to me, Ms. Prescot." Marissa gave her a skeptical look.

"I know what I am doing. Do you think Bess…Ms. Matthews would assign you to me if she thought I couldn't assist you in your choices?"

"Fire away with your questions but know that my patience is rapidly becoming exhausted." Marissa's lips curled into a tentative smile before she looked at her wristwatch. *Three more minutes.* She wantonly eyed the girl again. *This might turn out to my advantage.*

"Thank you. I can see by your clothes that you have impeccable taste. Are you looking to maintain that style?"

"If I wanted to do that, why would I be here? I want something that screams success, power, and money."

"I see. Do you want to incorporate the traditional reds and blacks, or do you have something else in mind?"

"Well, I think that if I want to say power those are good colors." Marissa picked up her coffee cup and took a sip covertly watching Elin over the rim. The girl certainly was attractive. Her mouth moved in ways that sent waves of pleasure over Marissa as she imagined the lips working their way over her body. She knew then that she wanted her and would have her.

After an hour of a lively and revealing conversation, Elin had a clear idea of what her new client needed in the way of business clothes. Because she was a partner in a venture capital firm, it was important that the woman look conservative and very professional, but Marissa wanted to go beyond the traditional banker image.

"Now that I have a very good idea of what your preferences are, Marissa, the next step is to arrange a time when will it be convenient for you to return and go over the selections that I picked out for you."

Marissa flipped open her phone and punched a few buttons. "What about Friday? I have meetings in the morning, but I could get away around three."

"That will be good." Elin wrote a notation about the appointment. "Thank you. Would you like me to write the date and time down for you?"

"No, I've already made a notation."

"Well then, I will be looking forward to seeing you this coming Friday. Come with me and I will show you out."

Marissa stood and followed her out of the room.

†

As Elin watched Marissa walk out of the shop, Bess came up behind her.

"How did it go? Was it as bad as you thought?"

Elin shook her head.

"I knew you could do it."

"Actually, it went really well. A bit shaky at the start because she was expecting you." Elin turned around blushing slightly before a smile crossed over her face. "Did you see her? Can you believe she is forty-three and a partner of a venture capital company? She certainly doesn't conjure up my idea of what someone in investments should look like."

"Remember the number one rule, dear...never mix business and pleasure." Bess shook her head and gave her a serious look. "It will only cause heartache in the end."

Elin hadn't disguised her sexual preferences and Bess didn't seem to have a problem with that. Although Elin had always known she was gay, she had never acted on those feelings in a relationship. She'd had her share of crushes and even dated a few women, but the extent of her physical experience was only passionate kisses with girls she had met and danced with in lesbian bars. Her life had been all about excelling in her work and she had little time for a social life.

She figured that once she proved herself in the designing world, she could devote time to finding a stable, permanent relationship. And, maybe, come out of the closet to her family.

"Trust me, Bess, I know the rules. She's more than twenty years older than I am. I can't see me in a relationship with someone that old." Elin screwed up her face. "It would be like dating my mother. And that idea is gross." She saw the look of humor on Bess's face and laughed. "Of course, you are not in that category, Bess, for you are still a young chickie."

"Okay, if you say so. I can't wait to tell Frank that someone thinks I am a *chickie*." Bess waved off the comment with her hand.

"I just want to thank you again for the chance you gave me today." A sense of exuberance washed over her.

"You'll do just fine. Do you want to confer about the client?"

"No, I've got it but if I run into problems, you'll be the first one I ask for help."

Bess patted her hand. "Anytime."

The door opened, and both women turned to the next client.

†

Marissa Banks left the store with a predatory smile. She had watched the sway of hips as she followed Elin to the store's door. The shop girl would no doubt satisfy her every need and maybe some she didn't know she had. She grinned. *Yes, Elin Prescot will do quite nicely.* Her body was tense at the thought of what was to come. Her last conquest had ended several weeks earlier and she wanted—no, needed—a replacement. The naïve young woman would be the perfect distraction. She had noticed the light in the girl's eyes when Marissa had told her she lived an alternate lifestyle.

"Yes, she is batting for the right team and I am going to be the pitcher that throws her a fast curve ball."

Relationships had never been her strong point. She preferred to love them and then leave them wanting more. She, of course, never gave more. The hunt was her lifeblood much the same way she sought out investors. Marissa smiled as she remembered following what she thought was a nurse because she was dressed in scrubs into a hospital. An investigation revealed that she wasn't a nurse but was a resident, so she made an appointment for a physical. Research, patience, and charm had worked on every woman she went after. She never remembered anyone's name except for the select few she allowed back into her bed. She was certain Elin would succumb to her seduction. They always did. After taking her cell phone out of her purse, she pressed a speed dial number.

"Marcus, I need you to adjust my schedule for next week."

"Sure thing. What do you want me to change, Ms. Banks?"

"I need Friday at three open this week. Next week I'll need from one to three open on Thursday."

"Okay. You do know that Mr. Heath is scheduled at two on Thursday, don't you?"

Marissa bristled at the young man's comment. Heath was an eight-figure account and her most important biggest client, but she didn't like Marcus telling her something she already knew. "I am aware of that, Marcus, and that is why

I'm calling you. I will be back at the office in less than thirty minutes and expect that you will have taken care of the schedule change by then."

She raised a hand, a cab stopped, and she got in.

"Fifty-fourth and Park. If you get me there in ten minutes there is a twenty in it for you."

She would be at her office in less than a half hour and that would rattle Marcus. She grinned. By now, she would have thought he knew better than to question any of her words or actions. She also knew that Frank Heath would not be happy with the schedule change and Marcus would have to face his wrath. How she loved to play this game. Delicious.

"No problem, lady."

As the taxi weaved in and out of the heavy traffic, Marissa wondered if the cabbie would sell out his family for a fifty. The vehicle screeched to such a sudden stop that Marissa had to stretch out her arm and brace herself from lurching forward. After opening the door, she handed the driver the exact amount for the fare.

"Hey, where's the twenty you promised?"

"I said ten minutes not eleven. You lose." She opened the door and got out before slamming it shut. As Marissa walked briskly toward her building, she laughed as she heard the driver bellowing obscenities.

†

"Marcus, did you change the appointment?" Marissa smiled slyly knowing exactly what his response would be.

"Ms. Banks, I called his secretary and she said there was no way the appointment could be changed." The young PA followed her into her office.

Marissa turned around and eyed Marcus. "Did you ask to speak with Mr. Heath directly?"

"Ah, no, ma'am."

Marissa angrily flipped through her Rolodex and picked up the phone.

"Hi, Janet, this is Marissa Banks, I need to speak with Frank." She waited for a moment. "Frank, it is good to hear your voice too. Listen, I need to change our appointment for next week...Yes, I know you don't like changes but what if I made it worth your while?" Marissa had developed a voice that she knew dripped with sexuality mixed with persuasion. It always got her what she wanted. "What if we met at Rao's around eleven thirty? It will be my treat. We can discuss new acquisitions and the funding for them." Marissa laughed. "Yes, I know it's your favorite. Do we have a date?" Her face glowed with victory. "I thought so."

Marissa hung up the phone and turned to Marcus before piercing him with a cold stare. "You know when I hired you, I really wanted someone older with more experience. But I took a chance on you. It looks like I might have to reconsider that decision."

"But, ma'am—"

Marissa held up her hand. "I don't want to hear excuses. Go see if you can do something right and find the Holcomb file for me."

Marissa watched as Marcus closed the door quietly behind him. She grinned, recalling the dejected look on his face when she picked up the phone and called Frank directly. Priceless. His dejected hang-dog expression was exactly what she wanted to see. Either she'd mold him into precisely what she wanted or he'd be out of a job. She could not tolerate a PA that had no initiative. Her mind turned to her new target, Elin Prescot. A wolfish smile crossed her face.

"Ah, how I love the hunt." It had begun, and she knew exactly how to woo the shop girl. She'd done it more times than she could remember, but each one was a new challenge. Marissa wondered which was more stimulating, the hunt or the challenge.

CHAPTER TWO

For three days, Elin pored over catalogs and designs for the perfect look for her first real client, Marissa Banks. Banks's figure was the kind that designers designed for so there was no problem in finding a large assortment of the proper apparel. Elin knew exactly what she was looking for and rapidly flipped through catalogs, dogearing pages until she was satisfied.

Her enthusiasm increased as the week passed, and she bounced around the shop with a big smile, causing everyone to smile back at her.

"Elin, you bring me fond memories with all your preparations." Irene Witherspoon, a coworker, patted her on the shoulder. "I still remember my first client...Jennifer Wolcheski. She was so hard to please. I think of all my clients over the years, she was the most difficult, but in the end she became a good customer." Irene smiled.

"I can't believe how nervous I am." Elin motioned to all the catalogs and pictures she had strewn across the table. "I feel like a kid in a candy store when I look at all the different choices I have. But then I get this feeling in the pit of my stomach...what if she hates everything?"

"You will do fine. If you run into a problem just excuse yourself for a moment and find me and I will help you work it out." Irene patted Elin's hand. "Remember that although you are the expert, the client is always right." Both women laughed. "Sometimes, the hard part is convincing them that you just may know what is right for them."

They both stopped what they were doing when they heard the bell announcing that someone had entered the shop. Elin's eyes darted to the clock on the wall. A quarter to three.

"You don't think she's early, do you?"

"Wouldn't be the first time a client got here before their expected arrival time. You know Camille will greet whoever it is and make her comfortable. If it is your client she will come get you." Irene patted her hand. "Why are you so jumpy? It isn't like this is your first day."

"I should've been waiting at reception when she arrived." Elin stood and quickly headed for the door.

Irene reached out and held Elin back. "Stop. Take a minute to gather your composure before you go out there."

"What do you mean? She's here and she's expecting to see me. I need to go." Puzzled, Elin looked at her.

"You need to take a deep breath and relax. The client needs to see you calm and stress-free and not all flustered.

Camille will take care of her so let her do her job and come for you, not the other way around."

Elin took a deep breath and closed her eyes for a moment. "You're right." She could feel her heartbeat slowing.

Just then there was a soft tap on the door before Camille opened it and poked her head in. "Your client is here, Elin."

"Thank you, Cammie, I'll be right out." Elin turned to Irene. "I'm ready to go now."

"Good. Now go knock her socks off." Irene smiled fondly. "Elin."

"Yes."

"Good luck."

"Thanks."

†

Elin walked with purpose to the front of the shop and saw Marissa Banks speaking with Camille. Her stomach churned as she watched what she was certain was flirting between the two women. She lengthened her strides.

"Ms. Banks." Elin smiled and held out her hand.

"It's good to see you, Ms. Prescot." Marissa took Elin's offered hand and firmly shook it before letting go.

"I was just going to get Ms. Banks a cup of coffee," Camille said.

"No," Elin blurted. "I will take care of it."

"Oh, okay." Camille turned to Marissa. "It was nice seeing you again, Ms. Banks."

"Likewise."

"Please come with me, Ms. Banks. I have everything prepared." Elin had seen Marissa wink at Camille. Her roiling stomach fought with the composure she was trying to maintain.

"I am looking forward to seeing what you have selected for me."

When they entered the room, Elin motioned for Marissa to sit in a chair. "May I get you that coffee?"

"No, thank you. I am on a tight schedule so if you wouldn't mind, can you just show me what you've come up with?"

The smile on Marissa's face had disappeared. Elin's heart sank at the businesslike tone as she scrunched her face in concern. Marissa wasn't going to buy anything and she probably already had a date with Camille. No way. Determination overtook her.

"Certainly, I think you will be pleased. Let's begin, shall we?" Pulling out her first choice, she held her breath as Marissa's eyes scanned the picture.

Marissa's long tapered fingers ran over the linen fabric of the last suit of Elin's presentation. "Hmm, you know, I do believe you have come up with a very functional yet attractive wardrobe." She repeatedly tapped her fingers on the pages. "You've captured success, power, and money, which is exactly what I wanted."

Elin beamed. "Are there any you would like me to order so you can try them on?" Marissa had appeared to be very interested in all the selections, but Elin knew better than to put much stock in that. Customers were finicky and when it came down to actual selections, they tended to pick only one or two items.

"It is important in my business that I look professional at all times." Marissa flipped through the selections again. Her eyes glanced at the drawings and photos and tapped one finger on the folder. "You have managed to capture exactly what I have been looking for...professional, but with a flair that says so much more. I think the words would be, *very successful.*"

Elin held her breath wondering if she would turn blue before she got an answer.

"I'd like them all."

Elin's eyes widened. "All?"

"Yes." A warm smile appeared on Marissa's face. "At first, I had my doubts about you, Elin, but after this," she touched the presentation, "I know you are just who I have been looking for."

A swell of excitement and pride filled Elin. "Would you mind undressing, so I can get your measurements?"

"Certainly." Marissa stood, took off her skirt, and then began to unbutton her blouse slowly.

Elin watched as the blouse came off and couldn't help her blush as she noticed the swell of Marissa's nipples.

"We have a dressing room if you like. It's probably warmer in there." She watched as Marissa's fingers lazily ran across her chest as she lifted her blouse off. Elin grabbed the table for support. "You can leave your slip on." Elin regained her composure as she took Marissa's measurements and recorded them. When she looked at the final calculations she giggled.

"What is so amusing?" Marissa asked. "Is my body that funny?"

"No. No. Let me finish, then I will show you."

"I don't like being made to feel foolish."

The tone of the woman's voice scared Elin. *Damn.*

"It isn't what you might think." She held out the page she had written the measurements on. "See, here are the measurements I just took." She picked up a scrap of paper from the table and apprehensively handed it to Marissa. "And, here is what I had written down after you left on Monday. It's a little game I play."

Marissa rapidly scanned both documents and was surprised that Elin's earlier estimations were exactly what she had written. "I'm impressed that what you guessed at on Monday was spot on." Marissa quickly dressed then looked at her watch. "I really must be going."

"Shall I place the order then?"

Blue eyes turned cold again. "That is what I said, isn't it?"

"Yes, yes, it is. When would you like to come back?"

"Next Thursday at one."

"Great. I will be looking forward to seeing you then." Elin held out her hand and was embarrassed when Marissa reached for the door handle instead. "Goodbye."

The woman had already left. Elin followed her out the door trying to catch up to her but she couldn't.

†

Elin's shoulders fell as her body finally relaxed once the door closed, signaling that Marissa had left the shop. She jotted the time and date down in her appointment book with a puzzled look. Marissa had given that day and time without consulting her schedule. That was odd. Elin took a deep breath, and although she tried hard to stop, she couldn't hide what she knew was the relieved expression that crossed her face. Turning back to the smiling faces of her coworkers, she beamed.

"What a rush."

"I take it by your expression it went well," Irene said.

"My first real client and she liked everything." Elin's eyes widened.

"Everything? I have never had a client that liked everything," Bess interjected.

"Yeah, she wants me to order all of my selections."

"And how many is that? I remember you had a rather large folder prepared for your client." Bess had a stunned look.

"Well, there are eight business suits, five dresses, and of course all the accessories."

"She wants you to order all that?" Bess's eyes widened.

"Yes." She saw a look of doubt on her boss's face. "Is there a problem?"

"Oh, no, it is just that doesn't happen...ever...you know, when the client wants everything." Bess paused. "She even wants the shoes?"

"She said that it is her policy to buy everything together, that way she doesn't have to search around for shoes or scarves to match." Elin shrugged. "Well, I'd better get busy. She is coming back next Thursday afternoon for a fitting." She thought for a moment. "I better make sure Sarah will be here then to do any alterations."

"Well, run along then and place your orders so they will be here in time."

"I think I need to make a few phone calls," Bess said to Irene once Elin left the area.

"I would call Horne's first." Irene commented.

"Yes, that's what I was thinking too." Bess picked up the phone and dialed. She spoke for several minutes.

"Thank you, Emily." Bess hung up the phone and turned to Irene. "Well, she pays her bills and always buys."

"I sense a *but*."

"Emily said one thing that disturbs me."

"And that would be?" Irene asked.

"Barracuda." Bess shook her head. "I don't want Elin in a situation with someone who might hurt her."

"We've all had that happen, Bess. If it does happen to her, at least she has our support. I remember the first time a client devastated me."

"Yeah, so do I. Not a pretty picture."

"No, it wasn't. Did Emily say anything else?"

"Apparently, this Banks woman has been to all the shops, but only once.

"Well maybe this time she has found the right person. Elin is destined for great things. I think we both know that."

Bess nodded in agreement. "It's just that she is such a sweet trusting kid that—"

"You want to protect her." Irene interjected. "Guess it's the mother in us that's coming out."

Just then, the phone rang.

"Hi Neil. Thanks for getting back with me. Listen, have you ever dealt with a client named Marissa Banks?"

†

Marissa felt like a pent-up cat as she paced her office before finally stopping and looking out the window to the street thirty floors below. Elin Prescot was preying on her mind and her body was reacting to those thoughts. She recalled how good it felt when Elin measured her breast. She leaned in close to wrap the tape measure around her and then the girl's fingers ever so gently brushed across her nipples. The remembrance of Elin's fingers lingering at the top of her thigh as she measured Marissa's inseam made her wet. *With such an eye for detail, I imagine she will be an attentive lover. Oh yes, Elin Prescot will do very nicely.* She would fall into her web never realizing what her fate would be. The thought of Elin Prescot languishing over her body while making love caused Marissa to close her eyes to cover up the delight she was feeling. *Yes, she is just who I have been looking for.*

She needed relief and knew just where to find it. Picking up the phone, she dialed the familiar number of Rachel Brown, a former conquest who was always willing whenever Marissa needed her. "I'll expect you at my hotel room at nine."

"I can't tonight. I have plans," Rachel said timidly.

"Cancel them." Marissa waited impatiently as she paced back and forth.

"No, I can't, it's my parents' anniversary. I have to be there."

"Unacceptable, Rachel." She breathed in deeply in annoyance.

"Well, maybe I could leave early and meet you."

"I thought you'd see it my way." She knew that Rachel could never tell her *no* and mean it. Marissa knew she was in Rachel's blood and the woman would do anything to keep it that way.

Rachel certainly didn't compare to the young shop girl Marissa had her sights set on, but she would do for the weekend. A vision of Elin came to her mind. There was something about the girl that intrigued her. Wholesomeness. Marissa laughed inwardly. It has been a long time since she knew wholesome. She guessed that Elin was around twenty-five. She chuckled. The shop girl was young along with being nice and firm. She smelled good like soap and water. Wholesome, yes, she could become used to that.

"Not in this lifetime." Marissa laughed.

For the weekend, she would allow Rachel to satisfy her. Although Rachel was older and had let herself go in so many ways, she did have the most talented tongue and knew exactly how to use it. *Perhaps while she is licking my clit, I will do a bit of fantasizing.* It wouldn't be the first time she pretended that the person in her arms was someone else. Marissa picked up her briefcase and surveyed her office before walking out the door. She grinned thinking of what was to come once she was in her apartment.

†

The doorbell rang and Marissa opened it. "What the hell has happened to you?" she asked sarcastically. "You used to take care of your appearance. Now you look like a drowned rat."

"In case you hadn't noticed it is raining heavily and I had to park two blocks away." Rachel took off her coat and held it out.

"Just leave it on the floor and come with me." Marissa took Rachel's hand and pulled her toward the bedroom. "Get those clothes off and get in bed," she ordered.

Rachel complied.

Marissa took off her slacks and panties before crawling on to the bed and straddled Rachel's head. "This is where I want you all weekend. Do you understand?"

"Yes."

"Then get busy."

†

The key clicked in the lock and Elin nudged opened the door with her hip and entered her apartment. The day had gone remarkably well, and she wanted to share her good fortune with her parents. The subway ride to her small apartment in Tribeca hadn't dampened her feeling of elation over her first real client. Closing the door behind her, she felt Kati, her small gray cat, rub up against her leg.

"Hey, girl, mom had a great day today." She bent down, picked up the animal, and kissed its head. "How was your day?" She held Kati close to her as she made her way toward the telephone and picked up the receiver only to return it to its cradle. "If I call and tell them, I might jinx everything. I'd better wait until it is a done deal." She nuzzled the cat again. "You are a good listener. What do you say we get dinner ready?"

Elin took a bag of lettuce out of the refrigerator along with some leftover chicken. As she was preparing her salad, her mind drifted to the day and one Marissa Banks. She knew what she liked in the way of business clothes but wondered what she wore outside of the office.

"Hmm, maybe I can convince her to let me find her casual clothes. Hold on, girl, you need to get her business order done at work first," she said to Kati. Elin shook her head and put the completed salad in the refrigerator before going into her bedroom and changing her clothes.

She paced her apartment with visions of Marissa Banks crowding into her mind. Elin knew what she needed to get

28

rid of her pent-up energy. The best way she knew to do that was to get outside for a mile run. That would do the trick.

She stood on the sidewalk and wished she had taken the time to find someone who would share her wonderful news. In the past, her career and studies had always come first, but now, she wanted to pursue a relationship. *Maybe after my run I'll have my salad then clean up and go to that lesbian club down the street. Maybe Ms. Right is waiting for me there.* For a fleeting moment, the image of Marissa Banks filled her mind before she started jogging down the street.

†

Elin heard music, laughter, and women's voices after opening the door of the corner bar named Glitter. She noticed that the establishment hadn't changed much since she had been there seven months before. While she wove through the crowd to the bar, she made eye contact with various women and smiled at each one.

"What'll it be," the overly tattooed barkeep asked.

"Rum and coke. Can you make that diet coke?"

"Sure thing."

"Well hello, beautiful. I don't think I've seen you in here before."

"Excuse me?" Elin glanced to her right and saw an attractive blonde standing next to her. She looked over her shoulder to see to whom the woman was speaking and realized that no one was there. She turned back and blushed. "Are you talking to me?" She placed her hand on her chest.

The woman smiled and in a low sultry voice said, "Yes, I am, beautiful. May I buy you a drink?"

A glass slid in front of Elin. "I already have one."

"You want anything?" the bartender asked the pretty blonde while giving her the once over.

"Corona and I'll pay for the lady's drink." The woman reached in her back pocket for her wallet, took out a twenty, and placed it on the bar.

"Thank you," Elin said with her eyes slightly downcast.

"You're quite welcome."

"You know you are wrong." Elin smiled shyly. She noticed the questioning look. "I have been in here before, but it has just been a really long time."

"Ah, that explains it then. I know I would have remembered someone like you."

"What exactly does someone like me look like?"

The woman seemed to be undressing her as she gave her an appraising stare. "Beautiful."

Elin touched her cheeks and felt the heat rising. Her eyes darted around the bar as she tried to think of something to say. This kind of flattery was far out of her experience. Finally, she held out her hand.

"I'm Elin Prescot."

Taking the proffered hand and holding it firmly she replied, "Chris Chambers."

"It's nice to meet you." Still, Elin was at a loss for what to say or do. "I...I guess from your comments you come here often."

"Not really...well, I guess every Friday would be often." Chris laughed heartily. She took a long swig of her beer. "I usually stop by after work for a beer or two and then go home." A blush covered her face. "I don't usually do this," she said as she motioned back and forth between them with the bottle.

"Do what?"

"Buy a beautiful lady a drink." Taking another long pull from the bottle she added, "Truth be told, you are the first." She shrugged then looked away.

The feeling of being special floated into Elin's heart and mind. She couldn't recall a time that anyone had made her feel that way. "I'm glad."

"Hey, do you hear that song?" Chris cocked her head.

"Yes." Elin recognized the soulful voice of Elvis Presley singing 'Love Me Tender.'

"I know it is sappy, but that is my all-time favorite." Chris took Elin's hand. "Dance with me."

Elin felt herself floating on air as she allowed Chris to lead her onto the dance floor and surround her with her arms. She closed her eyes, delighting in the sensations surging through her as their bodies moved as one to the music.

For the next two hours, Elin and Chris shared information about each other. For Elin, it was exactly what she had hoped for when she left her apartment earlier that evening. Chris was wonderfully attentive and very interested in everything that Elin had to say. When Elin shared the news about her big sale, Chris pulled her in for a big hug and then kissed her lips. The kiss was soft and gentle, and Elin hoped there would be more. She wasn't disappointed when, while dancing again, their lips met in what deepened into a very passionate kiss. As the night wore on Chris was so close to Elin that there wasn't any space between them.

"Is it okay to kiss you again?"

Elin did not refuse and several minutes later both women found themselves gasping for air.

Chris stood and held out her hand. "Come with me."

Elin looked at Chris. "There isn't a song playing."

"I don't want to dance." Chris laughed and leaned into Elin. Her hot breath tickled Elin's ear. "I want you to take me home."

"I don't have a car."

Again, Chris laughed. "Take me to your home where we can get more comfortable and get to know each other much, much better." She ran her hand high up Elin's thigh.

Elin suddenly understood the meaning of her words. "You mean you want to take me to bed?" she said in an incredulous tone. "We just met."

Chris pulled back with a glare. "So, what do you think this was all about?" She gestured between them. "You don't come into a place like this lookin' for long-term, babe. You come lookin' to get laid."

Elin didn't know what to do or say. She had come to this bar hoping to meet someone that she could develop a relationship with and not for a one-night stand. "I...I...I think you misunderstood."

"Oh, I don't think so. Your kisses said more and that is exactly what I want." She grabbed Elin's hand roughly. "Now, let's go."

"No," Elin said loudly, trying to wrench her arm away from the increasingly strong grip.

"Is there a problem?" A tall Amazon-like woman appeared out of nowhere. She looked pointedly at Elin and then at Chris who still held her arm tightly.

"Yeah, this bimbo led me on all night and now won't put out," Chris said angrily.

"Thought I heard the word *no*," the Amazon said. "In this place, it means NO." She reached over and wrapped her large hand around Chris' wrist squeezing hard until the grip on

Elin's arm ended. "Go on," she said looking at Elin. She glared at Chris as she tried to speak.

Elin didn't need anyone to tell her twice. She quickly got up and headed for the door. Her insides were quivering as the cool night air assaulted her, but all she could think about was getting home before she threw up. Once she was out on the street, she ran the short distance to her apartment building. Looking back toward the bar, she thought she caught a glimpse of Chris, but couldn't be sure. She took the stairs two at a time until she reached the door and unlocked it quickly. Safely inside, she climbed the old wooden staircase to the second floor and her apartment and opened the door. Finding herself in the safety of her own surroundings, she bolted the door and refrained from turning on the lights. If Chris had followed her, she would be looking for the lights to show as a sign of where Elin lived. She'd keep them off for the rest of the night.

Kati's body seemed to wrap itself around Elin's ankle, trying to get her attention. Elin picked up her baby and nuzzled her nose into the soft grey fur.

"Hey, girl, mom had a close call tonight." Elin shivered. "Guess a bar isn't the best place to find true love. I wonder where else I can go these days to find someone that is nice and doesn't want to get me into bed first thing?" With that thought, her stomach began to churn violently, and she headed for the bathroom.

†

Marissa arrived at her office earlier than usual on Monday morning. A wicked smile crossed her face as she imagined the look on her PA's face when he realized he was not there to greet her. Marcus prided himself on being there early with everything at the ready for her. *It will certainly start his week off on the wrong foot.* She laughed. *Bet after today he will start coming in at six.* Satisfied with how the morning would evolve once her PA arrived, she sat down at her desk and twirled her chair, so she could look out the window. The street below had a smattering of pedestrians while cabs and buses hurried down the street to their appointed destinations.

The weekend had been exactly what Marissa needed. At first Rachel was hesitant to commit to spending the entire weekend at the hotel with her, but as always, she saw the situation the way Marissa wanted. Rachel certainly had satisfied all her sexual needs and none more so than when Marissa fantasized that Elin was touching her and not someone else. A smile crossed her face as she closed her eyes in the remembered bliss of her imaginings...

Rachel rose up from between Marissa's legs and quirked her head. "I don't think I have ever elicited such a response from you before," she said.

"You didn't," Marissa said from her sexually satisfied haze.

Rachel moved up and then sat up straddling Marissa. "Oh really," she said grinding her center against Marissa's stomach. "Who else is here?"

Marissa rolled over on her left hip to topple Rachel. "I need a shower."

"I'll join you." Marissa gave her a searing look of disdain. "What? Do you want me to leave?"

"What part of 'you are to spend the weekend' didn't you understand?" Marissa's eyes bore into Rachel.

"I thought—"

"You're not here to think," Marissa interrupted.

"I'm sorry." Tears began to cascade down Rachel's cheeks.

"You know how much I love you being here with me. No one makes me feel the way you do." Marissa pulled the woman in close.

"Really?"

"Believe me, baby, there's no one like you." Marissa kissed her lips hard. "I really need a shower. Why don't you order us something from room service?"

"Okay," Rachel said in a small childlike voice.

"I think a rare steak would be nice." Then Marissa slid off the bed and headed for the bathroom.

"If Elin can excite me like that in a fantasy, I can only imagine what it will be like in person." Marissa said to the room after Rachel left.

…Marissa turned back to her desk and flipped through her day planner before developing a strategy to seduce the young shop girl.

†

Elin arrived at the shop earlier than usual. She had an appointment at nine with a new client and wanted to make sure everything was prepared. The experience with Marissa Banks had buoyed her confidence and she hoped her newest client would also place a big order. She had a satisfied smile on her face as she unlocked the door and went inside.

"Well you're early," Bess said with a smile. "Good morning. How was your weekend?"

"Good morning, Bess." Elin trembled when she recalled her weekend. *No way do I want her to know how stupid I was.* "Quiet would best describe it. How was yours?"

"What's wrong? Are you okay?" Bess asked with concern in her voice.

Elin looked at Bess trying to find the words that would make her look less foolish. Right then she felt like a teenager who was sneaking back into the house, trying to hide something from her parents. Bess had always been kind to her and in a way, she was her mother away from home. *Do I dare tell her about what happened?*

"I…I had a lapse in judgment, that's all."

Bess eyed her for a long moment. "And?"

"It was so awful." Elin couldn't help the moisture that began to fill her eyes. Her hand swiped away the threatening tears.

Bess quickly moved closer to Elin and took her arm.

"Let's go to my office. I think you could use a nice cup of tea first and then we can talk."

The office was warm and cozy, reminding Elin of a room in her grandmother's home. She didn't know if it was the tea or the ambiance, but she knew she was safe. "Thank you, Bess."

Bess patted her hand and sat in a chair next to Elin. "Why don't you tell me what happened."

"Well…" Elin's cast her eyes to the floor refusing to look into her boss's eyes. "I thought it was about time to get out and see if there was someone out there for me."

"Did you?"

"I thought so but…" As she related the events of Friday night, she realized how foolish she had been, and not wanting to see the disapproval in Bess's eyes, she looked away.

For her part, Bess listened in silence although her concern for Elin grew as the story unfolded. The girl was so naïve with a heart of gold and she could easily become an innocent victim out of sheer ignorance. Bess really didn't know what to say when she saw the mixture of shame and sorrow on Elin's face, so she gave her a hug.

"Are you okay?

"I feel so foolish. I should have known better."

"We all make mistakes, Elin. The important thing is the lesson you learn from those mistakes."

"Oh, I learned the lesson all right. Never go into a bar and let someone sweet talk me."

Bess could only shake her head for she knew that Elin still did not understand how the world of predators operated.

"Elin, I have never seen anyone who can see a person and know exactly what size they are as accurately as you do." She smiled fondly. "You need to know how to do that with people. How to judge their intentions and words."

"I do that," Elin said defensively.

Bess arched an eyebrow.

"I just expect everyone to treat me like I treat them," she said softly. "Why are people so cruel?"

Bess lifted Elin's chin, so they would be eye to eye. "They do it because they can, sweetie. Learn from this and the next time you are in such a situation, remember, and act accordingly."

"Oh, don't worry about that. I will never put myself in that position again. Feeling like an idiot is something I never want to repeat."

Bess could only smile at the innocent remark.

"Unfortunately, dear Elin, you will again because that type of person is all around us. You need to always be vigilant." She patted Elin's hand again.

"I wish that wasn't true," Elin whispered.

"So, do I." Bess gave her a quick hug. "Do you feel better?"

"Yes, thank you. I needed to share that with someone. Thanks for being here for me."

"Anytime." Bess got up. "We have a busy day ahead of us. You have Mrs. Blanchard and I would imagine some of the Banks order will begin arriving today." A chill ran up Bess's spine as she remembered the word *barracuda* was used to describe Marissa Banks. *Predators abound.* She sighed before she left her office with Elin to begin their workday.

CHAPTER THREE

A long, tapered finger casually tapped in a number as a slight smile crossed Marissa's lips.

"Good morning, Boutique La René, this is Irene Witherspoon, may I help you?"

"Good morning. This is Marissa Banks. Is it possible for me to speak with Ms. Prescot?"

"Why yes, Ms. Banks, just give me a minute to find her."

"Thank you." Marissa drew large concentric circles on a piece of paper as she waited.

"Good morning, Ms. Banks, this is Elin. How may I help you?"

Marissa scrawled DELICIOUS across the paper when she heard the young woman's voice. "Ah, yes, Elin. Thank you for taking my call. I'm sure you are busy."

"I'm never too busy for you," Elin said happily.

Her pen continued to have a mind of its own. LUSCIOUS

"Is it possible to change my appointment to eleven on Thursday?" Marissa paused, "That is, of course, if it doesn't inconvenience you too much."

"Of course we can change the time."

FIRM she wrote in bold letters.

"Thank you so much." Marissa smiled smugly. "You're sure I haven't caused any problems with this change?"

"No, none at all."

MINE. She smiled at the last word appearing on the paper.

"Great, you are a lifesaver. See you at eleven tomorrow then."

"Yes, see you then. Bye."

Elin hung up the phone and sighed and looked over her schedule again. She had lied to Marissa Banks. Late in the previous week she had promised a co-worker, Cybil Duncan that she would sit in on her consultation with a difficult client. Because the Banks account was a big one for the shop there was no way she wanted to jeopardize that. The account was far too important. She would have to work something out. She looked around the room, saw Cybil, and took a deep breath. She had better get this over with.

"Hey, Cybil, do you have a moment?" She waited until her co-worker looked at her.

"For you? Of course. What can I help you with?"

The bright smile and warmth on Cybil's face made Elin feel guilty as if she'd betrayed Cybil. She hadn't. What she was doing was what was best for Boutique La René.

"I have a bit of a scheduling problem." She saw Cybil's smile fade. "You know the client I have that bought everything?"

"Yes," Cybil said softly.

"Well, she just called and needed to change her appointment from tomorrow afternoon to the morning."

"What about Mrs. Eberly? She will be here at eleven-thirty."

"I know," Elin said softly. "We've spent the better part of yesterday afternoon and most of this morning mapping out strategies for Ms. Eberly's ensemble. I think you will do just fine now that you have a firm plan in mind."

Elin knew that Betsy Eberly was head of an advertising firm and had been an important client for years. Since she had last visited the shop, she had put on significant weight, which constituted the need for a completely new wardrobe. The problem was that the woman thought her style should stay the same.

"Is there any way we can change the appointment?" Elin asked Cybil.

"Let me see if I understand this. We have set a time and plan for my client, but yours wants to change times so mine must accommodate her?" The look of irritation on Cybil's face was unmistakable.

"The Banks account has the potential to be very lucrative for the business," Elin countered.

"Eberly already is."

Elin closed her eyes in resignation, understanding that she had made a terrible mistake.

"Look, I'm sorry. I didn't think. I just thought we could work everything out, but I can see now that I have made a complete mess of everything." She shook her head. "I will call Ms. Banks back and tell her that eleven will not work out."

"Didn't you already tell her the time was all right without consulting me?"

"Yes," Elin said dejectedly.

"You need to understand how things work around here, young lady," the matronly lady said testily. "You think you can just come in here and take over and be the big shot since Bess dotes over you."

Cybil's voice was loud enough for Bess to approach the women.

"Cybil, you will have to keep your voice down. Is there a problem?"

"I'd say so," Cybil said angrily. "Little Miss Goody Two-shoes here thinks that she can just change times without consulting anyone." She took a deep breath. "We have worked all morning and a good part of yesterday on the Eberly account and now, because her client wants to change times, mine gets cast aside."

Bess looked at Elin. "Is this true?"

"I really didn't think it would be a problem," Elin said stiffening her back. "Ms. Banks called and needed to change her time tomorrow. Since she is a new client and potentially a very big one, I thought it best to accommodate her." Elin tried to put a positive spin to her decision. In truth, she chastised herself for being so thoughtless of Cybil's needs. "I'm really sorry, but Ms. Eberly *is* Cybil's client, not mine. I was just helping her figure out a strategy to get the woman to understand that, since she's gained weight, the clothes that used to fit her body type years ago, don't now." She took in a calming breath. "Ms. Banks is *my* client and she is the one I need to accommodate first."

Bess looked between the two women before fixing her eyes on Cybil. "You know she is right, don't you? Putting a client first has always been the rule here. If Elin's client needs to change the schedule, then she should accommodate her."

"So, it is okay for her to throw me under the bus?"

"Cybil, how many years have you been working with Ms. Eberly?"

"Seven. But—"

The owner held up her hand. "I should think in seven years you know your client well enough to deal with her alone."

"You don't understand. She has gained an enormous amount of weight and—"

"And you will deal with it." Bess eyed Cybil. "From my observations, you and Elin have come up with a workable plan for Ms. Eberly. I think you can present that yourself, and if you need help, I will gladly sit in with you." She then turned to Elin. "Will you please go to my office and wait for me?"

"Yes." Elin left the room.

"I knew you'd take her side. She's your little pet." Cybil looked at the retreating Elin and scowled.

"Enough," Bess said in a voice that brooked no further discussion. "You've worked here for fifteen years and, in that time, you've dealt with all kinds of customers. Deal with Ms. Eberly, Cybil, and stop trying to get someone else to do it for you."

"Fine. She'll get what's coming to her," she mumbled before she turned around. "You know you can't keep rescuing her."

"I never have, Cybil. Mark my words, she's the genuine article and will outshine us all."

"Yeah, right."

Bess watched Cybil walk away and her mind turned to Elin who was waiting for her. What was she going to say to the young associate? Bess's heart went out to Elin who was such an innocent that she never fully understood that Cybil was a user and not someone to cross. She was extremely adept but had a habit of using the other consultants for her own purposes. Unfortunately, Elin had made the decision that her client was more important and for Cybil that was the kiss of death. It seemed to her that Elin attracted all the predators. As she walked toward her office and Elin who was waiting for her, Bess could feel the need to protect her from the world.

†

Elin, startled by Bess's dismissal, wondered what was going to happen as she walked slowly to the office with her head bent. She knew she'd really screwed up big time and felt like she was being sent to the principal's office.

Five minutes later, Bess entered her office, closed the door, and eased down in the chair next to Elin.

"Don't worry about Cybil. I'll take care of her if she tries anything against you."

"I honestly thought that my client should come first."

"You were right to think that. Nevertheless, you should have consulted with Cybil before changing the time. It is common courtesy, but I do understand your reasoning."

"I know I should have asked her, but in my defense, I was thinking about my client and not hers." Elin shrugged. "Which would you have chosen as the most important?"

"I understand your reasoning, but…" Bess shook her head, "I should have told you the histories of the women who work here, but in my position, I didn't think that would be wise. I'd rather you form your own opinions. I will, however, suggest you order a bouquet of flowers for Cybil. It will go a long way in saying you're sorry."

"I'll do that immediately." Bess was frowning. "Have I done something else wrong?"

"No, no." Bess shook her head. "Elin you need to be careful dealing with people both in the shop and elsewhere. Try not to be so open and accommodating."

"I know." Elin bowed her head. "My mother didn't want me to move here because I'm too trusting. I don't know how to be any other way."

"How about you just be a bit more cautious in dealings with people." Bess drew in a deep breath. "Just so you know, I have made some discrete inquiries about Marissa Banks."

"Why?" Elin's eyes widened at the revelation.

"Because we've never had anyone that wants to buy everything, and I wanted to find out if she could pay."

"Can she?"

"Yes, but there is something else you should be aware of." Bess's voice was kind but firm. "She never returns."

"What do you mean?"

45

Bess let out a slight laugh. "This is the only order she will make with you. There is no potential that there will be a big account for the shop. None at all."

"How do you know that will be the case with me? Maybe she just hasn't found the right consultant until now?" Elin countered.

"You may be right. That is something you will have to find out for yourself. I hope for your sake it is true. But now you are sounding like you are full of yourself, Elin. Yes, you did something no one else has done in this shop, probably in the city, but that doesn't mean it will always happen. If you bask in only one accomplishment, what more will you strive for, Elin?" Bess's voice softened. "Perhaps I should have told you about Ms. Banks sooner. I'm sorry I didn't."

"No, you shouldn't have. Like you said, I need to figure out people out on my own. I will try to do that, but I'm not sure I know any other way to act than be trusting."

"Perhaps you can learn to look beneath what is presented to what is. Most people show you what they want you to see and not who they are. That is why we find ourselves feeling cheated when we see who someone really is." Bess could see Elin's face flush in what she thought was embarrassment.

"How do you make that distinction, Bess? How do you know?"

"Experience." Bess leaned in and put her arm around Elin's shoulders. "I've been in the business for a lot of years and people still surprise me. As you go along you will pick up hints about how to judge people and it will become easier. I promise."

"Thank you, Bess, for everything. I understand what you are saying and will try to have a more critical eye when it comes to people. It won't be easy but I will give it a go."

46

"You're welcome. Now go order those flowers."

CHAPTER FOUR

With the ringing of the small bell over the door, Marissa Banks entered the shop. When Elin's face lit up in a brilliant smile, she felt a stirring of arousal. She moved toward the young woman with an outstretched hand.

"Ms. Banks, it is so good to see you. All your selections are here and I'm sure you will be pleased with how they will look on you."

"Marissa...remember?" Marissa fought the urge to smile when she heard Elin babbling as a cute blush washed over her face and neck.

Elin's face reddened even more. "Yes, sorry."

Once again Marissa took in Elin's firm supple body. She appraised the shapely figure, letting her eyes linger on the perfectly formed breasts. Her wavy brunette hair kissed her shoulders before cascading down her back. In some curious way set it off her azure-blue eyes and full ruby-red lips. Marissa resisted licking her own lips for want of the girl. She squashed her arousal.

"Shall we start?"

"Yes, please come with me."

Once Marissa was in the fitting room, Elin introduced the seamstress.

"Ms. Banks, this is Sarah Hamilton who is our expert in making clothes fit perfectly."

"Pleased to meet you. May I call you Sarah?"

"Certainly." Sarah looked at Elin. "Shall we begin?"

"By all means."

Elin never left the room during the alterations, keeping her eyes glued to Marissa's body—it was exquisite. At one point, Marissa lifted her eyes and Elin saw them rake over her body before she smiled and winked. Elin swallowed hard and resisted the urge to cross her legs while her body reacted to the look.

An hour and a half later, after Marissa had tried on each outfit and Sarah had marked them for alteration, the seamstress left the room. Elin let out a sigh of relief.

"I know how trying alterations can be, especially with all the outfits you ordered. I hope that was painless for you."

"It wasn't painful at all." Marissa smiled.

"I've moved your order to the top of the list, so we should have everything ready for you by next week. Do you want to set up a time for a final fitting?"

"I will get back to you on that." She looked at her watch. "Right now, I need to get going. I didn't realize how late it is. I will have to eat on the run if I am to make my one-thirty meeting."

"Would you like to share my sandwich?" Elin looked around to see who said those words.

Marissa cocked her head and grinned. "I wouldn't want to inconvenience you."

"Oh, no, you wouldn't be. I usually pack two sandwiches." She shrugged and felt her face redden again. "I'm a big eater. You can take one with you."

"I would love to share lunch with you. I think I have enough time to eat here since I won't have to fight the crowds to order something."

"Excellent. Please come with me to my office and we can eat there."

At first, each woman sat in silence. Elin could feel Marissa appraising her with sideways glances and it made her body tingle.

"This is delicious," Marissa said. "Is that Gouda cheese with the ham?"

"Yes." Elin could feel her heart sink when she saw Marissa wrinkle her nose slightly. "You don't like it?"

"On the contrary, it is my favorite cheese."

"Oh." Elin closed her eyes and let out a breath. She changed the subject. "I could see from your expressions that you were pleased with the results of the clothes you tried on."

"Hmm, yes I am. You have a good eye for fashion, Elin, which has proven fortunate for me."

Elin could feel her face heat up. "You seem to have made me blush more than once today."

Marissa laughed. "That is a first for me. I can't recall anyone ever blushing on my account." She cleared her throat. "In case you wondered, it looks good on you."

"Oh, no, that means you noticed it before." Elin's hands covered her face before parting her fingers slightly. She spied Marissa's face, which looked thoroughly amused. "You must think I am a real goof."

"No, not at all. I remember one time when I was younger, about your age, I was making my first big purchase, and I was so nervous that I snorted. Talk about being embarrassed. I think my face must have turned scarlet."

"Did you still seal the deal?" Elin laughed. The thought of the stoic woman blushing was completely out of her realm of thinking.

"Yes, I made the sale. Fortunately, my *faux pas* happened after we had signed on the dotted line." Marissa looked at her wristwatch again. "Look at the time. I really need to go."

"Oh, dear, I'm sorry I kept you so long."

"I completely enjoyed every minute." Marissa reached over and touched Elin's hand.

Elin, taken aback by the unexpected touch, could feel a surge of excitement spread throughout her body. Like an electricity surge rendering her unable to breathe. She didn't recall a time in her life that she had felt the sensations the touch had elicited. She was so enthralled in her thoughts, that she didn't realize that Marissa had risen and was about to leave the room.

"I will call you and set up a time for the follow-up appointment," Marissa said softly.

Elin jerked her head up wondering how Marissa had gotten to the door. Finally, the words made it through her muddled brain. "I will look forward to your call." She stood and went to where Marissa was standing.

Once again, Marissa reached out and touched Elin. "Thank you for sharing your lunch with me. Now, I must really go."

Elin stood there with her mouth open, wondering what had just happened. She turned back to the room and looked around, trying to recall every minute of the last several hours. On the table, she saw her folder and a check attached to the outer cover, confirming that Marissa had indeed been there She looked down at her hand half expecting to see red marking the spot where Marissa had touched her for it certainly had been searing enough to leave a mark. *What's happening?* She couldn't get the vision of Marissa Banks out of her mind.

†

Elin approached Bess and held out the check.

"She has paid the balance. Is that normal?"

"Generally, no, but sometimes they do...not often though."

"Even before they get their clothes?"

"Not really. Generally clients wait until they have the completed order." Bess looked at Elin curiously. "Do you think there is a problem?"

"No, I don't. I was surprised, but since this was my first sale I didn't know any different."

"We all worry about our first order, dear. You hit the trifecta the first time out which is astounding. Trust me, in all my years of experience I have only had one full order, but only because two outfits were all that was ordered."

"I'm sorry, Bess." Elin lowered her eyes and felt foolish for asking the questions she had.

"For what?"

"Sometimes I don't think before I say the stupidest things."

"Don't we all?" Soon Elin was joining Bess laughing. It didn't take long for the laughter to end and Elin to take on a rattled look. It was the same look Bess had noticed when Elin shared the story of meeting the girl at the bar.

"What's the matter?" Bess asked. For a long moment, Bess waited for the rattled Elin to say something. She had seen Marissa leave the shop with a very pleased look on her face that was different from that of a client who was happy with her purchases. No, this had been a predatory look of satisfaction and Bess remembered thinking that it was odd. Coupled with Elin's current agitated state, she could only surmise something had happened between the women.

"Nothing." Elin smiled slightly.

"How did the fitting go?"

"Fantastic. The size was almost perfect, and the alterations are minimal." Elin smiled. "If the look on her face when she tried them on was any indication, I'd say she was pleased."

"You know, we had an intern years ago that one of the customers was not very nice to." Bess needed to find a tactful way of finding out the reason for Elin's anxious look.

"Really? What happened?" Elin cocked her head to the side. "Was she hurt?"

"Yes," Bess nodded. "Mentally not physically. The woman kept calling her stupid and threatening to tell me.

When it became physical, she finally confessed what was happening."

"Did you call the police?"

"There was no way to prove anything since this was back before surveillance cameras were readily available. So we ended up refusing to do business with the client."

"That's awful. How could anyone do such a thing to another human being?" Elin wrapped her arms around her waist and shivered.

"If anyone does that to you, Elin, you will tell me, right?"

"Of course."

"Good. Why don't you take your lunch now?" Bess smiled. She hadn't expressed her suspicions about Marissa Banks but she had sown the seeds.

"Oh, I already ate. I think I will check in with Cybil and see how her meeting went and if she needs any help." She looked questioningly at Bess. "Will that be okay?"

Bess desperately wanted to ask when Elin ate lunch but decided against it. "Yes, I think Cybil will appreciate your concern. The meeting went well, but Ms. Eberly was a bit subdued with the realization of what her weight gain meant to her wardrobe."

Elin turned to find Cybil but swung back around to Bess. "She really is a very nice and funny person."

"Who? Cybil?"

"No, Ms. Banks."

"Oh. I'm sure she is." Bess just shook her head as the word *barracuda* swam in her mind. She would be there for Elin. Something told her that it wouldn't take long.

CHAPTER FIVE

Marissa entered the meeting room with only a few minutes to spare. She greeted the investors gathered for her presentation. She had spent too much time with Elin Prescot but the results had been worth it. The look on Elin's face when she left the fitting room was exactly what Marissa hoped it would be. When the time came, the shop girl wouldn't be able to resist her.

While the others on the team presented their findings, Marissa's mind drifted back to the attractive brunette and the feelings that had stirred in her. She hadn't expected her body's extreme reaction that touching her caused. While sitting in the testosterone-filled room, she smiled, knowing that they would never know the soft sweetness of Elin in their arms. *She will be mine and want no other.* Marissa could feel the tightening of her center as Elin continued to dominate her thoughts. The young shop girl was so tantalizing that Marissa considered changing her plan and taking Elin earlier than she had anticipated. But, in the past, her plans had always been successful, so why change a winning formula.

†

Friday proved to be slow for Elin as she waited nervously for the call from Marissa to set up their next meeting. Butterflies fluttered in her stomach in anticipation of hearing the woman's voice once more. As hard as she tried, she just couldn't keep her mind on the tasks at hand, as Marissa kept teasing the edges of her conscious thoughts. There was something there that she couldn't quite grasp the meaning of, and that alone distracted her the most.

"Elin," Bess said for the second time. "Hey, where is your head?"

As if she were languishing in some dreamscape, Elin could hear her name but felt helpless to respond. Not until she felt a firm hand touch her arm, did she finally respond and look dazedly at the boss.

"Oh, Bess, I'm sorry, did you say something?"

"Are you okay?"

"Of course. Why do you ask?"

"Well, there is that quizzical look on your face and the fact that I've been trying to get your attention for about five minutes."

"No. You haven't, have you? Really?" Elin asked the question but knew the truth. Bess had caught her daydreaming. "Sorry, I was trying to visualize the right colors for Karen Blanchard. She is proving difficult because she doesn't fall completely into any one category."

"Don't you hate when that happens? Would you like an ear to bounce ideas off? I can't guarantee I will have the answer, but I have had my share of quirky clients."

Elin, glad that she was able to give a palatable reason for her lack of attention, smiled at Bess. The truth was that she didn't really know what was going on in her head. She only knew that there was something lurking there that she couldn't fully understand.

Just then, the bell over the door jingled and both women looked to see who was coming through the door.

A man with a small vase of flowers entered the store. "I have a delivery for E. Prescot," he said.

"That's me." Elin gave Bess and then the man a shocked look. "Who would send me flowers?" She approached the fellow and took the bouquet in her hands. She fumbled in her pocket, found two dollars, and handed them to him. "Thank you."

"Well, well, Elin. It looks like you have an admirer. Have you found that special someone?" Bess asked.

"No. I haven't a clue why I got these. It must be a mistake." She sat the vase on the counter, snatched the attached card and slid it partially out of its envelope. What she read brought a broad, delighted smile to her face. *Thanks for sharing. You can make me lunch anytime. M.*

"Well," said Bess. "Don't keep me in suspense. Who are they from?"

Elin looked up and quickly shoved the card back in the envelope and put it in her pocket.

"My parents. They wanted to congratulate me on the Banks sale." She didn't know why she lied, but something told her that clients sending flowers was a no-no. Bess was already suspicious enough of Marissa and she didn't want to add to that.

"Well, they are beautiful and absolutely perfect." Bess bent to smell their fragrance. "Your office is going to smell fantastic."

"Yes, they are." Elin smiled broadly. "My problem is how I will get them home. The subway on Friday afternoon is not really suited for transporting a vase of flowers."

Bess smiled and shook her head. "Only you, Elin, would think of that. Why not treat yourself today and take a cab?"

"Good idea. Well, I should get back to figuring out Ms. Blanchard. I promised Cybil I would get back to her by the end of the day." She picked up the vase and took it with her to her office. Once she closed the door, she breathed in all the wonderful smells emanating from the beautiful flowers. Bess was right; they were perfect. She took the small envelope out of her pocket, pulled out the card and ran her fingers over the writing. That couldn't be her handwriting. She opened Marissa's folder and looked at the copy of the check. Marissa's writing was bold and precise while the writing on the card was small and indistinguishable from countless other scripts. She then noticed that the address and phone number on the accompanying receipt was that of Marissa's business. *That's curious.* She picked up the phone and entered the phone number.

A man answered the phone. "This is Marissa Banks's office. May I help you?"

"Yes, this is Elin Prescot and I would like to speak with Ms. Banks. Please."

"She can't be disturbed at this time. If you would like to give me a message, I will pass it on."

"Oh." Elin hadn't expected this response. "I see. If you could just tell her 'thank you' for me I would appreciate it."

"Will do," was all the man said before the line went silent.

Elin ended the call and chastised herself for being foolish. "I should never have called her. That guy must think I'm some sort of weirdo." She lightly tapped her forehead. "Maybe she'll call me back."

†

Marissa's PA, Marcus Saunders, looked up when she came to his desk.

"Any messages?" Marissa asked absently.

"Yes, one."

Marissa took the message, read it, and chuckled softly. *It is working. Excellent.* "Marcus, this woman will call again next week...probably on Thursday. I do not want to speak with her. Is that understood?"

"Yes, ma'am."

"Even if I am standing right here in front of you, I do not want to speak with her." Marissa looked the young man squarely in the eyes. "Don't mess up on this or it will cost you your job."

"I understand. You can count on me, Ms. Banks."

"See that I can."

Marcus watched his boss turn for her office without further comment and bristled with irritation. He had seen the look of victory on her face before when she closed a big deal. He had also sat by and watched as she played mind games with various women. She had never before put his job on the line. There was something different this time in her voice. It was as if she were afraid to speak with the caller.

"Get a grip man—she isn't afraid of anything or anyone," he mumbled. On the other hand others, including himself, seemed to find her terrifying. He recalled the voice of Elin Prescot. When he said she couldn't speak with his boss, it rattled her. From the sound of the voice, she was young, and obviously not in tune with the ways of the business world if she thought she could just call and speak to the boss at once.

Ms. Banks had given him his orders and he would not fail. His job was paying the bills and he needed it. Still, he resented her making him be the go-between with her conquests.

"One day it will come back to bite her in the ass," he whispered before he smiled. "I hope I'm still here when it happens."

†

When Elin arrived at work on Monday, she went in search of Sarah to find out how the alterations on Marissa's clothes were going.

"Sarah, there you are. I've been looking for you."

"Good morning to you, too," the seamstress said stiffly.

"Oh, I'm sorry." Elin closed her eyes embarrassed by her actions before looking directly at Sarah. "I really am sorry, Sarah, if I've hurt your feelings. I was being rude and you don't deserve that." Elin lifted a shoulder. "Good morning, Sarah, how was your weekend?" Elin laughed self-consciously.

"My weekend was good. The children and grandchildren came by as usual for Sunday dinner after Mass." A smile crossed Sarah's face.

"How are they all doing? The last time we spoke your youngest granddaughter, Felicia, was having her tonsils out."

"Thank you for asking. You always remember each of my children and grandchildren's names. Felicia is doing well." Sarah's face brightened.

"That is wonderful to hear." Elin flopped down in a chair next to where Sarah was seated at a sewing machine. "I need to know how the Banks alterations are coming along so I can give her a date to come back for the final fitting."

"I was in on Saturday and did much of the work. I think that I should have it all done by Wednesday, or Thursday at the latest."

"Great. Thank you so much." Elin sighed. "You know, this is my first really big sale, so I am anxious that it go just right."

"Anxiety is written all over your face, Elin. Don't worry, it will all work out. She seemed very nice and I could tell she really liked you."

This had been the first person that spoke kindly about Marissa, so Elin warmed immediately to the remark. "Really? You don't think she is someone I should be cautious of?"

Sarah turned in her chair and moved it closer to Elin. "I spend time with every client that comes in and buys so I have seen my share of good and bad people." She smiled affectionately. "I judge people by how they treat me. Often, they are mean-spirited and disrespectful because they think I am nothing but a lowly seamstress. But this lady seemed sincerely respectful of my position. And, when you briefly left the room, she had only praise for your abilities. I don't think you have anything to fear from her."

Elin couldn't help the vibrant smile that emanated from her face. Marissa was not someone to fear as Bess lead her to believe, but a warm, kind person.

"Thanks, Sarah. I needed to hear that."

†

"Bess, do you have a minute?"

"Certainly." Bess looked into Elin's face and saw concern along with something else—disappointment. It encompassed her face. "What can I do for you?"

"Sarah told me yesterday afternoon that the clothes for Ms. Banks were ready. I've been expecting her to call to set up a time for the final fitting. What should I do? Is it okay to call her? Or, should I just wait?" Elin twisted her fingers nervously. "I don't want to bother her, but Sarah worked overtime to get them ready." She shrugged. "Do you think I've messed up somehow?"

A nagging apprehension gnawed at Bess. She would be glad when Marissa Bank's business with the store was complete and out of Elin's life.

"What were the arrangements you made with her?"

"She said she would call me. That was last Thursday. I keep expecting her to call but so far, she hasn't. You don't think something has happened to her, do you?"

"I doubt it. She is probably just busy." Bess had never had a client make a partial payment let alone a full one and never return, but she wouldn't put it past Marissa Banks. There was something just not right about the woman. Bess didn't like the way she looked at Elin when she first came into the shop.

"Why don't you give her until tomorrow afternoon, and if you haven't heard from her you can give her a call." Bess was just acting like a foolish mother hen.

"All right," Elin said nervously. "I just don't want to—"

Bess held up her hand and shook her head. "Don't worry it will all work out."

"But I need to make sure Sarah is available."

Bess' heart went out to Elin. She remembered how anxious she had been with her first big sale. "You know, dear, we have all been there and we all survived."

"What do you mean?"

"We all have successful conclusions to our first big sale and you will be no different. Trust me, it will all be fine." She drew Elin in for a light hug. "Stop worrying."

"I'll try."

†

By two o'clock on Thursday, Elin was a nervous wreck. Marissa hadn't called for an appointment. Elin couldn't shake the feeling that she must have done or said something wrong to make Marissa not call. Again, thoughts and feelings for Marissa played on the edge of her consciousness. Now it would be her responsibility to make the first move. Secreting herself in her workroom, she placed a call that had her insides all a flutter.

"This is Marissa Banks's office. May I help you?" the male voice announced.

"Yes, this is Elin Prescot. I would like to speak with Ms. Banks about an appointment I need to make with her."

She heard the man's sharp intake of breath.

"I don't see your name anywhere. When is the appointment exactly?"

"No, you misunderstood. I don't have one. I need to make one."

"I see," the man said in a matter of fact tone. "Is this relating to a financial concern?"

"No, it's personal." Elin didn't think that she should be discussing Marissa's clothing purchase with the man.

"I see," he said again. "Ms. Banks is booked solid through next week. The earliest appointment I can give you is two weeks from today."

Elin didn't know what to say or do. The man obviously was doing his job and she, at the same time, didn't want to violate Marissa's confidentiality.

"Do you want me to set up the appointment for you?" the man asked impatiently.

"No." Elin took a deep breath to gather her composure. All the stress of waiting for the call had caught up with her and she felt her body tremble. "Will you please ask her to call me at 555-8274. It's important that I speak with her at her earliest convenience."

"Certainly. Will there be anything else?" he asked gruffly.

"No."

"Thank you for calling."

The line then went silent and the tears that brimmed around the edges of her eyes began to fall.

†

"Excellent, Marcus. There is hope for you yet." Marissa scooped up the message with the number and went to her office.

Everything was going just as planned. She looked at the clock on her desk and noted the time. She'd call her back just before five. A feral smile crossed her face.

"Hmm, Elin Prescot, you are about to have the ride of your life."

Several hours later, Marissa dialed the number and was pleased to hear Elin's voice. "This is Marissa Banks, may I please speak with Elin Prescot?"

"Speaking." Elin let out a breath she had been holding. It seemed like forever until she heard Marissa's voice.

"Elin, darling, I am so sorry that I haven't been able to get back to you before this. The market was doing strange things this week, requiring my full attention." She heard Elin sigh. "Will you forgive me for my tardiness?"

"Yes."

Marissa smiled when she heard the coolness in the one syllable answer. "Please don't be angry with me," she said in her most conciliatory voice.

"I'm not. I was just worried I had done or said something wrong."

A broad smile crossed Marissa's face. *Perfect.* "Not possible. I really am sorry. Can we make an appointment for tomorrow?"

"The man I spoke to on the phone said you were booked solid," Elin countered.

"I was, but I've rearranged my schedule and I can be there by five tomorrow afternoon. Will that be a good time?" Marissa knew that the shop closed at five, which fit perfectly into her plans.

65

"I am not sure Sarah can be here at that time. If there are any changes that we need to make, we should schedule for next week."

Marissa heard the dejection in the girl's voice and smiled. "Not to worry about that. If need be, I will come back next week. Listen, I am really anxious to have the clothes, so if it won't be too inconvenient for you, can I come tomorrow?"

Elin sighed again. "Tomorrow at five will be fine."

"Perfect. Thank you so much for understanding." She paused then added, "Elin, you're the greatest."

"I'll see you at five tomorrow then."

Marissa heard the softening of the voice and knew she had achieved her goal. "I'm looking forward to seeing you again."

†

"Excuse me, Miss," a man said as he knocked into Elin.

"Sure, it's okay," she said several moments later as she looked around, wondering who she was talking to. Ever since Marissa left the store a week earlier, she had found herself daydreaming more and more about the woman during her subway ride home each evening. With glazed eyes, she watched as the landscape whiz by, taking very little note of where she was until she realized the train was about to pull away from her stop.

"Please let me by, this is my stop," she said frantically. Once her foot touched the platform, she shook her head and sighed deeply. "What is going on with me?" Her dazed condition continued as she walked to her apartment. Not until she unlocked the door to her apartment and Kati rubbed up against her leg did she realize she couldn't remember walking to the building or climbing the stairs.

The last seven days had her fixed on one thing only— Marissa Banks. She hadn't slept soundly or eaten much since her last encounter with Marissa. When she called earlier that day, she had felt anger and jealousy that Marissa's job interfered with her calling sooner. Elin couldn't deny the warm feelings she had when she heard Marissa's voice, and the pang of sadness she felt when Marissa hadn't recognized her voice. A vision of Marissa invaded her mind as she stood stroking Kati while she watched children play in the street below.

"She certainly is quite charming, Kati. Did I tell you how funny I think she is?" She lifted the cat to her face and kissed its fur gently before placing her on the floor. "Well, she is." Elin shook her head as she tried to summon up a thought that still refused to surface. Marissa was beautiful, talented, and charming. Something just beneath the surface of the woman intrigued Elin. The attraction that she felt was increasingly difficult to deny—Marissa Banks captivated her.

Elin walked to the small kitchen table that held the bouquet that Marissa sent her. Many of the petals were drooping and some, she suspected, had fallen on the table from Kati swiping at them. She bent slightly and breathed in the delicate scent of the flowers. Her mind again turned to Marissa. There was something about how the cool eyes seemed to be picking her apart with delight that made her want to know more. Marissa exuded danger and that had a draw all its own.

"For heaven's sake, she's old enough to be my mother."

Once again Elin found herself at the window looking down at the people passing by. Her eyes trailed to two women walking hand in hand down the street.

"I want that," she whispered. "Is that what it is like to be attracted to someone? Holding hands, unaware of who else is there, not caring what they think?" She walked over to the couch, sat down, and flicked on the television. Silently she welcomed Kati who jumped up and nestled next to her. She mindlessly stroked the cat while blankly looking at the screen. Marissa played on the edges of her mind again, taunting her to realize a truth of which she was not aware.

"If only I could figure out what it is. Maybe when I see her tomorrow I will understand," she whispered to Kati.

Later that evening, she woke on the couch with a start. It was midnight and she hadn't eaten or showered.

"I've got to get a grip." Getting up, she went into the bathroom, showered, then went to bed. *Tomorrow is a big day.* With that thought in mind, she drifted into a fitful sleep.

CHAPTER SIX

Bess's concerned eyes focused on a haggard-looking Elin. "Do you want me to stay with you while she is here?"

"No. No, I will be fine. You are having the kids over for dinner tonight and don't need to be here babysitting me." Elin smiled. "I'm just really nervous...you know... first big sale and all."

"Is that all?" Bess looked skeptically at the girl.

Elin took a deep breath and closed her eyes, wishing Bess would just disappear.

"I have to admit that your constant warnings about Marissa have me rattled."

Bess's eyes widened. "Oh no, please don't feel that way."

Wearily Elin closed her eyes again. "I really don't know how else to feel, Bess. Frankly, I haven't seen any indication at all that Marissa is anything other than sincere." She opened her eyes and fixed them on her boss. "Yet you keep telling me to be careful."

"It's only because I have seen far too many people in my life that prey on others." Her eyes searched Elin's. She smiled fondly. "It's my mother hen coming out. I care about you and want to protect you."

"I don't need to be protected, Bess." Elin gritted her teeth. "I am twenty-six years old. I pay rent, have a job, and even can go to the bathroom alone." She squeezed Bess's hand. "I know I haven't been out in the world as long as you have but I think I have a pretty good handle on life and people. I know you worry about me but please trust me. I will be okay."

Elin's shoulders relaxed and she gave Bess a smile. She knew she had exaggerated about having things under control. At the moment that was something she'd rather not share. "Are we good?"

"Yes, we are good." Bess realized she had crossed a line after hearing Elin's angry retort. "I do trust you. I also care about you, Elin. It's that mother hen thing." She didn't really trust Elin for she could feel there was more to the story but at that point she had no other choice but to end the conversation.

"You have my cell number if you run into any problems or need help. It won't be a problem to come back if you need me." She patted Elin's arm. "I need to go now. Please don't hesitate to call me."

"I won't. Have a great weekend," Elin said anxiously.

"Same to you." Reluctantly Bess left. "Be safe, Elin," she softly prayed.

†

Marissa stood outside Boutique La René and watched Elin pace in the shop. Occasionally the young shop girl would swipe at her eyes. Marissa smiled. She'd worked this scenario enough to know exactly why Elin was crying and inwardly she patted herself on the back. She checked her wristwatch. Five fifteen. Perfect. Elin turned and went into her office and soon returned with her coat and purse in hand.

"It's time." With a triumphant smile, she walked quickly toward the door when she saw Elin look up.

Once Marissa opened the door she said, "I am so sorry I am late. I had a client that just wouldn't leave."

"I thought you weren't coming," Elin said, her voice trembling before her eyes found the floor.

Marissa engulfed her in a hug. "Oh, I am so sorry to have caused you concern." She stepped back a bit and lifted Elin's chin before she gently wiped the tears away. "Did I cause that?" she asked.

Elin stepped farther away.

"No. I didn't sleep very well last night, and it has been a really long week."

"Would you rather do this next week?"

Elin's eyes widened, and she blurted, "No! Please, I have everything ready and you did say you were anxious to have the clothes."

71

"Okay, but only if you're sure." At that moment Marissa's body tingled with what she knew would be another victorious conquest.

An hour later, Marissa had tried on all the clothes.

"Absolutely wonderful. Everything is perfect."

"Thank you. I'm so happy that you are pleased with the choices and the fit. Please just give me a minute to finalize everything for the shop's records."

While Elin sat at the table and began the final paperwork, Marissa took in her long-tapered fingers and imagined them stroking her. She closed her eyes relishing what the moment would be like.

"We can send them out to your residence if you'd like."

The words brought Marissa out of her reverie and she smiled. "Not necessary, Elin, I have a service standing by to come and get them. Can I take up just a little more of your time?"

Elin had a puzzled look and Marissa surmised that the young girl's mind was whirling with muddled thoughts of what was to come. *She doesn't want me to leave. How sweet.*

"You can have all the time you need," Elin finally said.

"Good." Just what she wanted to hear so Marissa picked up the phone. While placing a call to the delivery service, Marissa smiled while her eyes seductively scanned the firm taut body. The erotic memories of her reaction when she fantasized that Rachel was Elin came back to her.

"Okay, they will be here in five minutes." A shiver ran through her body as she remembered how it had felt when she held the young girl in her arms earlier. "I was thinking that you might let me take you out to dinner." She cocked her head. "It's my way of saying *thank you* for all you've done for me."

"You really want to have dinner with me?" There was a definite tremble in Elin's voice.

"Of course. Why wouldn't I?" Marissa pointedly let her glance linger on the girl's breasts.

"Well for starters, I am sure you could come up with someone who is more mature and sophisticated than me. I'm not very worldly. Most of my life I've had one goal and that was fashion."

For a long moment, Marissa gazed at Elin. The girl was different from anyone else she'd ever met. She was unassuming, completely open, and naïve. *Until she's been with me and then she will never be the same again. My god, is she a virgin? This will be bliss.* "You have no idea how very special you are. Do you?"

Elin shook her head and looked away.

Marissa gathered Elin in her arms and held her close. "There is no one else I'd rather be with." When she peered into the smaller woman's gaze, she saw what she hoped to see. Slowly and purposely, she lowered her head to touch Elin's lips gently. She pulled back slightly.

"Will you please have dinner with me?"

"Yes." For a second Elin's mind flitted to Kati and whether there was enough food before she felt Marissa's lips. All else was forgotten. Never had she known such bliss in the simple yet erotic kiss. She knew in that moment that she would always crave Marissa and the way she made her feel. For the first time in her life she was floating on a cloud that she had no intention of getting off.

CHAPTER SEVEN

Dinner, at the elegant Olica Restaurant inside the Kimberly Hotel, with Marissa was like a dream come true for Elin. The French cuisine along with red wine was everything she had ever dreamt about romance. Marissa was charming, solicitous, and made Elin feel completely at ease. When they spoke, Marissa's eyes focused on her, making her feel as if she were the only person in the room.

"Oh, the meal was marvelous. Thank you so much for everything," Elin said.

"No, thank you." Marisa reached across the table and took her hand. "Until you came along, I had no idea how lonely and boring my life had become."

"You have a way of making me blush." Elin was certain that her face had turned scarlet.

"I like how it looks on you."

Elin was way out of her element and for a fleeting second a sense of foreboding filled her mind. Marissa was like no one else she had ever met, and she desperately wanted to have a relationship with her. Slow down, girl, don't do something you will regret. With that thought, she knew she needed to distance herself. "Will you excuse me for a minute?"

Marissa let go of her hand. "Certainly. Don't be too long. They will be bringing the dessert tray soon."

Elin got up and walked toward the ladies room, frantically trying not to turn around and run back to the table.

"What the hell am I doing?" she whispered. She knew she was on a collision course with her destiny in the form of Marissa Banks. The woman was no longer playing on the edges of her consciousness—she had enveloped Elin fully.

As she returned from the ladies room, she felt the dark blue eyes that were appraising and wanting her. She was totally smitten with Marissa and wanted to know her in every way.

"I missed you," Marissa purred.

At that moment, Elin knew she was helpless to deny Marissa anything. She reached across the table tentatively and touched Marissa's hand. "I missed you too."

When the waiter arrived with the dessert tray and mechanically described all the delicious fare, Marissa's eyes searched Elin's. "Do you care for anything?"

Elin held Marissa's gaze. "No, nothing there appeals to me."

Marissa looked at the waiter. "Nothing, just the bill." Her gaze returned to Elin. "If none of those desserts appeal to you, what does?"

Elin cleared her throat. *What do I say now?* Instead of speaking, she let a slight smile play on her lips and lowered her eyes. Her face was hot, but not as scorching as the feelings that Marissa was creating throughout her body.

"Spend the night with me," Marissa said softly.

"My cat will be wondering what has happened to me," Elin offered. She lifted her head to look at Marissa. "I never stay out this late." Her gaze again fell to the table again. When she heard no response, Elin raised her head and saw the dark blue eyes beseeching her to stay. Her heart was pounding and every nerve in her body screamed out for a touch. She lowered her eyes.

"I've never..."

"Please spend the night with me. We won't do anything you don't want to." For Marissa, those words were strange for every woman she had been with always did exactly what she wanted. But Elin was different, and she would require special extra tender treatment.

"My cat..." Elin looked directly into Marissa's eyes.

"Will be fine."

A smoldering gaze ensnared Elin and she wanted nothing more than to find herself lost in it forever. "Yes, she will."

†

Elin expected they would go to Marissa's home and was surprised when she steered her into the hotel's elevator.

Marissa answered her questioning look. "I have a home in the Hamptons, but I have a suite here to live in during the week. The commute from the east end is terrible, and with my job being so stressful I figured I didn't need the extra hassle."

When they exited the elevator and stood in front of Marissa's door, Elin felt both panic and excitement. There was no doubt in her mind that being with Marissa was the right thing to do. The woman excited her as no other ever had, and she at long last wanted to make love. She had waited until the right person came along and she knew, without doubt, that Marissa Banks was the right person.

After closing the door and attaching the security lock, Marissa took Elin into her arms and lightly kissed her lips. Leaning back, she smiled mysteriously.

"Hmm, it would be so easy to get addicted to your kisses."

Elin wanting, no needing, to kiss her repeatedly, bent forward, but Marissa avoided her advances and took her hand leading her into the bedroom. Once again, she took Elin in her arms and hungrily started kissing the wanting lips. Elin offered no objection to the deep and passionate kisses, enthusiastically taking Marissa's tongue into her mouth.

Marissa pulled out of the kiss and slowly began to undress her. With each button that came open, she kissed the skin underneath. As Elin's blouse fell to the floor, Marissa stepped back and looked appraisingly at Elin's body.

"I've thought of you like this ever since I first saw you. Even with your slip I can tell that your body is all I hoped it would be and more." Elin closed her eyes when Marissa's fingers slid under the straps of the silk and lifted them so they would fall over Elin's shoulders before landing on the floor. Again, Marissa's gaze drifted to the body and the perfect breasts with taunt nipples that even the lacy bra couldn't contain.

"You are so beautiful," she whispered as she reached behind and unfastened the bra.

Elin flinched when the bra fell away from her body. Although she wanted this, it was strange to be standing there naked in front of Marissa, or anyone for that matter. She watched Marissa's expression change.

"Do you want me to stop?"

"No. No, that is the last thing I want." Elin let her arms snake around Marissa's shoulders to unzip her dress which joined the other garments on the floor. She leaned in and tentatively kissed a creamy shoulder. Her imagining of the moment paled in comparison to the actual event. The feel of the skin under her lips sent shock waves throughout her body and she wanted to feel more.

"Please, Marissa, make love to me."

A feral smile crossed Marissa's face as she picked the young girl up and laid her on the bed. "I've wanted to make love to you ever since I first saw you." Then she lowered herself over Elin's naked body.

Marissa gently stroked every inch of Elin as their naked bodies lay close together. She had never spent as much time with anyone to achieve an orgasm, and although that caused her concern, she went ahead at a slow tempo.

"Do you like how this makes you feel?" Marissa's fingers made their way down a sweat-soaked belly.

"Yes."

"And this," she purred. Her splayed, long tapered fingers leisurely touched Elin's wet center.

"Oh, yes." Elin closed her eyes, reveling in the sensation that the fingers were creating.

While her fingers tantalized, Marissa's mouth kissed the hollow in Elin's neck before her lips moved down to capture an extended nipple. She sucked softly at first then took in as much breast as she could and began kneading it with her mouth.

Elin moaned, arching her back, which encouraged Marissa to suck harder. At the same time, Elin raised her hips, urgently wanting to feel the long fingers inside her. When it came, her orgasm was long, hard, and sustained. Marissa's touch had her senses on overload and never in her life had she felt so completely loved. Just when she thought she had achieved the ultimate release, the woman's touch would electrify her to heights she never imagined were possible.

The spasms finally subsided, and Elin sighed when Marissa held her close, kissing her softly. She whispered, "Elin you are so beautiful. I have never felt this way before." Soon Marissa's lips found hers and they became embroiled in a deep soulful kiss.

Elin pulled away and held Marissa's face in her hands. "Will you teach me how to make love to you?"

Marissa smiled rakishly. She held off her own orgasm longer than she ever had before. She needed immediate relief. She took one of Elin's hands and led it down past the curly hair to her saturated center. She then placed her fingers on top of Elin's and guided them inside. Slowly she moved their fingers in short strokes then pressed their middle fingers against her *g* spot.

Raggedly Marissa said, "Always remember that spot." She then bore down hard on Elin's middle finger. Her orgasm didn't take long to materialize—she had been ready for it for weeks.

"Again," she commanded and held Elin's fingers inside her. Marissa's body stiffened as her hips moved rapidly to keep pace with the questing fingers. One powerful orgasm after another wracked her body unmercifully consuming every fiber of her being.

As she lay there wrapped in Elin's arms, Marissa wondered what had just happened to her. She couldn't recall holding anyone the way she was tenderly holding the younger woman. Her fantasies with Rachel paled in comparison to reality, and there was nothing in her recent memories to compare with the effect that Elin just had. The young girl was sleeping soundly in her arms and she wondered if this liaison was like all the others. Of course, it was—she never did longer than a weekend.

†

When Elin opened her eyes, she saw a sleeping Marissa lying close to her. Closing her eyes again, she vividly recalled the night before as her body reacted to the memories. Now, with clarity, she knew what her mind had been trying to tell her for the past week—she and Marissa were destined to be one. She snuggled closer and nuzzled her neck.

"Good morning."

She watched as Marissa's face at first looked like she was trying to figure something out before she smiled.

"Good morning." She then turned over and pulled Elin close. "I love waking up with you in my arms," she cooed. "Can you feel the connection between us?"

"Mm-hmm. Can we please make love again?"

"We can make love all day if you want." Marissa ran her fingers over bulging nipples. "I can start here and then when you want more, I can go," her fingers trailed down between her legs, "here." She slid a finger inside, then two. "How does this feel?"

Elin could only moan as she spread her legs wider and lifted her hips.

"I'll take that as a yes." Marissa then slid her fingers out.

"Please don't stop."

"Oh, I'm not stopping. I've just begun." Marissa gently rolled Elin on to her back. "I want you to feel everything." Her eyes raked over the naked body before her lips began their exploration with kisses that trailed down her body before her tongue began licking.

Elin gasped. Never in her life had she realized that her body could feel such things. Euphoria. Want. Need. Joy. Life was made perfect by Marissa loving her.

†

Marissa woke up but didn't open her eyes. It had been a long time since she had felt so rested. Elin was a wonderful elixir that she didn't know she needed. She stretched and opened her eyes. What she saw woke her completely. No one *ever* left her until she told them to leave.

"Where do you think you're going," she said angrily to the naked girl. What she hadn't counted on was the disarming smile on the girl's face or the predatory way she crawled up the bed.

Elin leaned in and kissed her soundly, then said, "I need to go home and take care of my cat." She kissed Marissa again, pulled back, and smiled. "I need to change my clothes. Day old panties are yucky."

Marissa turned her head away. "I was hoping you would stay the weekend."

"I'll be back. My parents always call on Saturday and if I'm not there they will panic." When Marissa refused to look in her direction, Elin touched Marissa's face.

Marissa slapped the hand away. "Stop."

"Please don't be angry with me," Elin pleaded. "I need to feed my cat and get clean clothes."

"Isn't there someone you could call to feed the cat?" Marissa had been in this scenario more times than not and knew exactly how to achieve the results she wanted. Some women needed the direct approach—you're not leaving—while others needed a guilt trip—that was this girl. What she wanted was Elin there, with her, for the weekend and that was how it would be.

"Well, there's Mrs. Wilkerson across the hall but she is old and doesn't get around very easily."

"You never know until you ask."

"But, Marissa, that doesn't solve the problem of my clothes."

Marissa squeezed her eyes and when she looked at Elin her forced tears were rolling down her face. "I was hoping that when I took your clothes off last night they would stay off."

Elin leaned in and held Marissa close. "I'm sorry. I didn't mean to upset you, but I have responsibilities."

Marissa's body stiffened.

"Then just go." Marissa pushed Elin away. "Just get out of here."

Elin reeled at the rejection. "No. I don't want to go."

Marissa got up out of the bed, walked quickly to the bathroom, and closed the door with a bang.

"What do I do now?" Panic filled Elin's mind as she realized that she had ruined everything. All she wanted to do was feed Kati and get a change of clothes. "Shit, what can I do to make things right. I can't lose her...not now."

She quickly sent a quick text message to her mother to tell her she'd call them tomorrow evening. Once she was home, she'd figure out what to tell her mother.

When Marissa came out of the bathroom, she was pleased to see Elin still naked and standing by the bed looking grief stricken.

"I thought I told you to leave," she said coldly while moving forebodingly toward the girl. Marissa stood so close to Elin that she could feel the heat radiating from the young woman's body.

"You don't really want to go do you?" She bent and repeatedly kissed Elin's lips lightly before her tongue parted them and entered. "Are you wet for me?"

Elin swallowed. "Yes."

"Show me what you're feeling," Marissa whispered. She saw Elin's look of confusion, took the girl's hand, and led it down her body. "Touch yourself and come for me."

Elin hesitated.

Marissa looked at her poised hand and nodded. "Show me," she demanded.

Elin looked helpless to do anything but comply as she slid her fingers through her slick wet middle before sliding them inside and kept her gaze fixed on the dark-blue eyes.

Marissa knew that the young shop girl would feel a heightened sexual rush knowing that she was watching her. It didn't take long before she saw Elin's eyes close as she cried out as her body erupted strongly in pleasure.

Marissa stood and watched as Elin removed her fingers. "Did that feel good?"

"Yes," Elin said breathlessly.

"Take your wet fingers and run them across your lips." Marissa saw the objection in the girl's eyes. "Do it."

Elin slowly began to run her fingers over her lips.

"Now lick them." It was not a request.

Elin gulped but complied.

Marissa watched in fascination as the girl licked every part of her hand. *This is like taking candy from a baby.* She smiled and seductively moved closer and let her tongue run lightly across Elin's lips.

"Hmm, I like how you taste. Do you want to feel my tongue lick your pussy like I did last night?"

"Yes." Elin was trembling with what only could be anticipation.

Marissa sat Elin down on the bed and spread her legs before she knelt on the floor and lowered her head between the girl's thighs and the soaked center. When she finished, she pushed Elin down on the bed before straddling her face. "Now, it's your turn."

When Elin eagerly complied, Marian knew she'd stay the weekend.

Several hours later both women were satisfied and laid wrapped in each other's arms. Elin breathed in the heady smells and sighed in deep satisfaction. "I want to stay here with you."

"What about your cat, your parents, and your damn underwear?"

"I will call Mrs. Wilkerson and my parents," Elin countered. "I just have a thing about wearing day old panties." She shrugged and looked pleadingly at her lover.

"Don't wear any."

Elin blushed. "I couldn't do that. It wouldn't feel right."

"Get up and put on your blouse then go sit in the chair by the desk," Marissa ordered.

Elin dutifully obeyed. "This feels funny."

"Close your eyes and pretend you are at work on Monday, the phone rings and you are told it is for you."

"Okay."

"When you answer you hear my voice and I ask if you are alone. What do you tell me?"

"Yes."

"Are you thinking about me?"

"Yes."

"Mmm, are you wearing any panties?"

"No."

"Touch yourself for me."

"I can't, not here."

"Sure, you can. Just slide your hand down between your legs." Marissa smiled when she saw the young girl comply.

"Are you wet?"

"Yes."

"How wet?"

"Very."

"Slide your finger inside." Marissa felt her arousal begin as she watched Elin's reactions.

"Does that feel good?"

The woman's voice captivated Elin. "Oh yes."

"Slowly slide you finger in further." Marissa got out of bed and stood next to Elin, watching and wanting.

"Make yourself come."

Elin's finger slowly began to slide in and out of the slick opening until the need overwhelmed her and she pumped harder. When she felt Marissa's finger join hers, she stopped.

"Don't stop," Marissa demanded. She straddled Elin's legs, grabbed the girl's free hand, and guided it to her own need.

†

Elin woke with a start not knowing where she was until she looked over and saw Marissa sleeping soundly next to her. *Is this real?* Stretching slightly and closing her eyes, she remembered the night before and Marissa's insatiable need to make love even in the showers they shared. *Yep, it's real.* She pulled the sheet aside and carefully got up.

"Where are you going?" a sleep filled voice asked.

"To the bathroom."

"Don't be long."

When she laid back down Marissa pulled her in close for a kiss. "Hmm this is perfect," she whispered before adding, "It's my turn." Marissa rolled off the bed to use the bathroom.

Sliding back under the sheets Marissa moved close to Elin. "Did you miss me?" she purred, breathing in deeply.

"I never want to lose sight of you," Elin said.

"All you have to do when I am not there is close your eyes and dream. There is always going to be this connection between us."

Elin's heart soared with the words. Never had anyone wanted or loved her so passionately. The word floated in her head as she captured Marissa's lips. Her hand ran over the full inviting breasts as her lips moved to a tempting ear lobe. Her tongue darted in and out of Marissa's ear then stopped.

"I'm in love with you," she whispered. "I'm in love with you."

Marissa had heard the words a countless of times and would always silently congratulate herself for the victory. But this was different—Elin was not like all the others. Her hands captured the young girl's face as her eyes searched Elin's.

"Let me show you how I feel about you," she said as she began a tender assault on Elin's willing body.

†

The two women stood close as Marissa's arm rose to hail a cab.

"Come with me," Elin pleaded. "Spend the night with me."

Marissa's arm snaked around the girl's shoulders. "I wish I could, but I can't."

"Why?"

"We've been through this already," Marissa said irritably. "We both have to go to work tomorrow, and if we

Erin O'Reilly

spend the night together, neither of us will be in any shape to do our jobs." Marissa laughed. "You've worn me out."

"You didn't seem so worn out thirty minutes ago in the shower." Elin leaned in closer. "Will you ride with me?"

"If I do that you know I won't let you go."

Elin smiled happily. "And that would be a problem how?"

"Not tonight." A cab pulled up to the curb. She opened the door. "Get in."

"Is something the matter?" For a moment, Elin frowned at the cool no-nonsense tone of Marissa's voice.

"Are you getting in or not," the cabbie growled.

Marissa guided Elin into the cab. "No." She leaned in and handed the man a fifty. "Make sure she gets there safely." She kissed Elin's cheek. "I'll call you," she said. "Remember, no panties," she whispered, "I love you." She pulled back from the cab, closed the door, and smiled at Elin.

Elin smiled back, then craned her neck to catch the last glimpses of Marissa as the cab wound its way through traffic. She leaned her head back, closed her eyes, and tried to relive each exquisite moment since Friday. *This is the greatest feeling on earth.* The cab pulled up in front of her building. She got out, walked up the stairs to her building, and went inside.

CHAPTER EIGHT

For Elin, going into her apartment with the lights out was strange. Normally she left a light on if she was going to be out after dark. Kati greeted her by wrapping her body around Elin's legs.

"Hey, girl, did you miss me?" She picked the cat up and carried her into the kitchen. "Good, you still have food and water." She went to the cabinet and took out a can of cat food. "Would you like a special treat for being such a good girl while I was away?"

Kati purred loudly.

"I thought so."

Once she had undressed and taken a shower, Elin curled up in her bed, debating whether to call Marissa and tell her good night or not. She picked up her phone then stopped, realizing she didn't have her number. She opened the search engine on her phone and searched for the number of the hotel and punched in the number.

Elin heard the greeting," may I help you" and said, "Marissa Banks' please."

"I'm sorry, there is a do not disturb for Ms. Banks. Would you like to be connected to voice mail?"

Elin felt a pang of sadness in her heart. "Yes, thank you." When she heard the beep she said, "I just wanted to tell you good night and that I love you."

Sinking underneath the covers, Elin closed her eyes and a vision of Marissa came to mind at once. The weekend had been glorious, and she knew that her life now would never be the same. Her body had been alive with the wants and desires that she had thought she would never experience. As she relived their first moment together, she felt aroused, let her hand slide past her belly, and began to moan.

†

"Good morning Bess," Elin said happily as she entered the store.

Bess always looked forward to Elin's smiling face in the mornings but this morning she seemed exceptionally happy. "Well, you certainly are in a good mood for a Monday morning."

"It is a beautiful sunny day, why not be happy?" Elin countered.

"Yes, indeed why not." Bess eyed Elin. There was something different about her and Bess was sure there is more to the story. She'd wait until Elin was ready to share. "I see the Banks woman paid in full. Were there any problems?"

Elin focused on her calendar avoiding Bess's eyes, fearing her face would give her away. "None at all. Everything was perfect." She squeezed her thighs tightly trying to stifle the sensuous feelings that coursed through her center at the mention of Marissa's name.

"Do you think she will be back?"

"Most definitely," Elin said confidently before adding, "she was very pleased with our whole operation. She said I...we were just what she had been looking for." She raised her head and focused her eyes directly on Bess. "See, you were wrong about her."

The daggers Elin's eyes were shooting in Bess's direction were unmistakable. Not wanting a confrontation, she decided to change the subject. "I see that Mrs. Blanchard will be in today. Were you and Cybil able to figure out the right colors for her?"

Elin sighed in relief as the subject of Marissa closed. It would be difficult to keep hiding her feelings for Marissa if she continued to speak her name. Bess was wrong about Marissa and one day she would tell her exactly how wonderful she was.

"Yes, we did."

"Good." Bess turned to answer the ringing phone.

Elin squeezed her legs tightly again and closed her eyes, hoping that the next words Bess would say were, "Elin, it's for you." She had felt undressed and vulnerable riding the subway in that morning, knowing she wasn't wearing panties. Elin, lost in her thoughts, didn't hear Bess calling her name.

"Elin, did you hear me?"

In anticipation, Elin felt moisture spread onto her inner thighs. "No, I'm sorry, I was thinking about an outfit for Ms. Blanchard."

"Well, that was her and she has to change her appointment until tomorrow." Bess looked directly at Elin whose face flushed. "Are you okay? You look like you might have a fever."

Elin touched her face and felt her hot cheeks. There was no way she was going to say that she was fantasizing about her lover. "No, I'm fine…too much sun I think." She shrugged as the feelings of arousal subsided.

For the rest of the day, Elin felt wetness rise then fall with each ring of the phone that wasn't for her. As five o'clock neared, she wondered if she should call Marissa. She really wanted to hear Marissa's voice, but she had said she would call and the last thing Elin wanted was to upset her lover. The thought of pleasuring herself at work as her lover directed her was appealing in a naughty sort of way. Elin longed to just connect with Marissa. After waiting for another hour, she finally closed the door for privacy and dialed the now familiar number.

"Marissa Banks's office, may I help you?"

"Yes, this is Elin Prescot. Is there any chance I might speak with Ms. Banks?"

"She has left for the day. Would you like to leave a message?"

Elin was devastated. "Would you please let her know I called?"

After she hung up, Elin rifled through the drawers in search of a phone book. Not finding one, she went to Bess's office but found the door locked. Everyone had left. She closed her eyes as she desperately tried to recall the number of the hotel but came up blank. When she got home, she'd call her. She went back to her work area to gather her belongings before leaving for home and the phone call she knew would brighten her day.

While sitting on a seat on the subway Elin mentally smacked her forehead and shook her head. She had the number of the hotel all along on her phone. She considered calling then but after looking at all the people around her decided against it. She looked at her wristwatch, noting she'd be home in twenty minutes. The time couldn't go fast enough for her.

†

Elin hurriedly put the key in the lock and opened the door to her apartment.

"I thought that was you I heard." Mrs. Wilkerson came out of her door. "Was your cat okay when you got home last night?"

Elin looked at her neighbor and remembered she hadn't thanked her properly.

"Yes, thank you so much, you were a lifesaver." She smiled brightly edging further into her apartment.

"That must have been one important meeting since you got in so late last night." Mrs. Wilkerson looked at Elin speculatively.

93

"It was." She wanted to get away, but she didn't want to be rude to the neighbor who had helped her out. "Listen, I would like to send you some flowers as a way of thank you."

"Don't waste your money." Mrs. Wilkerson just waved a hand. She then turned and went into her apartment and closed the door.

"Okay, I won't." Once she closed her door, Elin shrugged off her coat before going directly to the bedroom. It didn't take long to take all her clothes off and get under the covers in her bed. She held her phone and pressed the hotel's number and could feel the rise of desire building.

"The Kimberly Hotel. This is Randolph, may I help you?"

"Marissa Banks please."

"Just a moment," the man said politely. "Ma'am, Ms. Banks isn't picking up, would you like to leave her a message?"

Crestfallen Elin answered, "Yes, thank you." When she heard the beep she said, "Hi, it's Elin. Please call me, my number is 555-8049."

She longed for Marissa so much that all else didn't matter. She mechanically got out of bed, her arousal ended. She walked naked into the kitchen and put food in Kati's bowl and opened the refrigerator door for her own meal. "I'm not hungry." In her bedroom, she looked at her discarded clothes on the floor, then crawled back into bed and pulled the covers up around her neck. She clicked on the television, found the financial network, and scanned the crawl bar to see if anything unusual had happened with the market. It hadn't. She knew Marissa was a very important and busy person who just may not have had the chance to call today. Closing her eyes, she recalled speaking with her parents on Saturday while Marissa nipped at a nipple and her fingers stimulated the other. She couldn't get off the phone fast enough, so they could make love. She smiled at the thought.

"Marissa, where are you?" she whispered as her fingers ran down her belly before resting in wet, silky smoothness.

Just then her phone rang, and she looked at the display, disappointed to see her mother was on the other end.

"Hi, Mom, what's up?"

"It's more like what's up with you," Dorothy Prescot said. "Why exactly were you so eager to get off the phone yesterday? You've never done that before and we were worried."

"Mom, I was busy."

"Doing what?"

"If you must know, I was on a date."

"I called you this morning around ten and you still weren't answering."

"I wasn't home."

"Where were you, Elin? Still on your date?"

"If you must know, yes, I was still on my date."

"How wonderful, Elin, I am so happy that you finally have found someone. Tell me all about him."

Elin sucked in a breath. "Not him, Mom, it is her."

"A woman? You were on a date with a woman and spent the night with her?" Dorothy's voice held an edge to it. "How could you do such a perverse thing? We didn't raise you to be like that."

"Mom," Elin said evenly, "there is nothing perverse about how I feel. I am not interested in the gender but in the person. Can you understand that?"

"I understand about having things in common with other girls but to have sex with one…that is unnatural."

"It seemed natural to me," Elin countered, and then she could hear her mother crying. "Mom, please don't cry. Try to understand that she makes me happy."

"It is all too much to process right now. Let me think on it and I'll get back to you later this week, after I've sorted it all out and discussed it with your father."

"Fair enough. Mom, I love you."

"Okay."

Elin heard silence. Her mother had hung up and for the first time ever she didn't say "I love you too.'" She wiped away a tear and thought of Marissa and knew she had made the right choice.

†

Marissa's phone rang just as the stranger she had picked up in a bar once again didn't bring her to an orgasm. When she saw the message light flicker, she reached over, lifted the phone, and pressed the message button. She heard Elin's message and a satisfied smile crossed her face.

"You're really tense. Want me to try again?" the nameless woman asked.

"No. Get your clothes on and get out," Marissa demanded.

"Hey, it's not my fault you can't unwind."

"Get out."

"Fuck you," she screamed as she put her clothes on.

Marissa's eyes bore into the stranger. "You just tried to do that and failed every time. Now get out."

Once she heard the door slam, Marissa's thoughts returned to the message she just heard. "Ah, young sweet Elin, you were so unexpected...so eager to please...so open to everything...so luscious...so inventive..." She closed her eyes and could feel her body react to the thought of Elin. "I don't think I ever had a virgin before. Oh, sweet young Elin, it is such a pity." She then reached down, slid her fingers through the slick wetness, and entered. Her orgasm was immediate.

CHAPTER NINE

Elin walked quickly into the shop and on to the room where she and Cybil would be working with Carmen Blanchard who, she knew, was difficult. Bess was in the room speaking with Cybil.

"Sorry, I'm late. I didn't sleep too well last night and then I overslept."

"I hate when that happens. It messes up the entire day." Bess smiled and whispered, "You didn't get here before your client and that's not good. Go put your things away, and I'll tell Camille to bring her back." Bess looked at her. "Be prepared, Mrs. Blanchard can be quite critical."

"I know, Bess. I messed up."

"Just be careful."

After Bess left, Elin took in a deep breath and looked at Cybil who was scowling.

"Well, it's nice of you to finally show up," Cybil chastised from her seated position in the room. "From your past actions of throwing me under the bus where Mrs. Blanchard is concerned, I shouldn't be surprised."

"Sorry. Like I said, I overslept. I understand that the client is here and Camille will be bringing her back."

Camille, with the client standing beside her, rapped softly on the doorframe and smiled.

"Good morning Mrs. Blanchard. Please come in." Elin stood and held out her hand. "It's nice to see you again. May I offer you a cup of coffee?"

"I'd like to know why it is," she looked at her wristwatch, "ten-o-five and you are just now getting around to seeing me. My appointment with you, Cybil, was for ten o'clock on the dot."

"Mrs. Blanchard, it was my fault. Cybil had nothing to do with being late. I overslept and even though I paid for a taxi I still didn't get here until ten. I am so sorry for making a problem for you. Can you forgive me?"

"Let's just get this done with so I am not late for my next appointment. You may leave me and Cybil alone, Ms. Prescot, I won't be needing your input."

†

From that point forward, the week deteriorated for Elin. She kept having problems with everything she did. It was fortunate for her that the other women in the shop were there to rescue her. She was the last to leave each day as she waited in hopes that Marissa would return her calls. Not wearing underwear and feeling wetness each time the phone rang became a normal occurrence. Each day she called both Marissa's office and hotel, leaving the same message: please call me. Nothing had been the same since Marissa had entered her life and showed her what true love was all about.

"Elin, I'm leaving," Bess said to the girl, who had her head bent over an order sheet. "You've stayed late every day this week. It's Friday, why not go home on time today."

Elin lifted her head and smiled at her boss. "I'm just finishing up the Blanchard order for Cybil so I can fax it to the fashion houses. I won't be long."

"You do know that the Blanchard account is Cybil's. I think you've atoned for the mix-up by now. Let her do her own work from now on. Okay?"

"I will. I told her today that I was done helping. She called me a traitor." Elin let a small smile cross her lips.

"Don't let her get to you, dear."

"I'm trying, Bess."

"Will you look at that rain coming down? I didn't hear any weather report about rain." Bess frowned. "Do you want me to do that for you?"

"No, I'm almost finished." Elin fed the papers into the fax machine and pushed send. "Have a great weekend, Bess." Elin returned to the task.

"You too. Try and get some rest. You've looked really tired all week. Lock the door after me and take one of our umbrellas with you."

"I will." Elin watched Bess leave, then dutifully locked the door and pulled the shade. Going back to the desk, Elin picked up the phone and dialed the number that was now etched into her brain.

"Marissa Banks's office. May I help you?" the familiar male's voice asked.

"This is Elin Prescot. Is there any chance I might speak with Marissa today?"

"She is unavailable."

"I see. Will you tell her I called?"

"Yes." She heard the man sigh and clear his throat. "Listen, no matter when you call here next, she will be unavailable to you."

Elin sucked in a sharp breath.

"Do you understand what I am telling you?"

Several moments passed before Elin could speak.

"Yes," she finally said tearfully before hanging up.

†

Marcus Saunders sighed; he hated doing his boss's dirty work. Elin Prescot seemed so genuine and nice, but he had his orders and he would follow them—his job depended on it. He tapped softly on the door and waited until he was told to enter.

"I'm leaving for the day. Is there anything else you need me to do before I go?"

Marissa looked up at the young man, then to her watch. "You're leaving rather early, aren't you?"

The man looked uneasy. "Don't you remember I requested to leave early today? You told me it would be okay."

"I don't recall that conversation at all. Are there any messages?" The scowl on Marissa's face was unmistakable—she wasn't happy.

"Just one," he answered dejectedly.

"Did you set her straight?"

"Yes. She seems like a really nice—"

"If you want to keep your job you won't say another word." Marissa glared at the man.

"Is there anything else?"

"No."

Marcus turned to leave.

Marissa added, "You don't leave until I do."

He desperately wanted to challenge her, but he knew if he did, he would be out of a job. He would have to cancel his doctor's appointment and make it for a time when it didn't interfere with his boss's schedule.

†

Marissa got up and locked the door. As she sat down, a predatory smile crossed her face. She picked up the phone and dialed 555-8274. When she heard Elin's voice she purred, "Are you alone?"

"Marissa." She heard the quiver in Elin's voice and knew that her body was trembling with anticipation and desire. She smiled.

"Are you alone?"

"Yes," Elin whispered.

"Do you have panties on, sweet Elin?"

"No."

"Hmm, I like to think of you sitting there all wet and needy. Are you wet for me?"

"Yes."

"Mmm, touch yourself. Tell me what you are doing."

"I repositioned myself in the chair and have pulled my skirt up and spread my legs. Now I'm sliding my fingers inside.

"How wet are you?"

"Very."

"I bet you are dripping. Am I right?"

"Yes."

"Taste yourself for me. I remember how good you tasted on my tongue."

Marissa heard Elin groan.

Marissa smiled. "Now, slide three fingers inside, curl them, and squeeze them hard."

"Oh, god." Elin quickly erupted.

"Squeeze hard and move your fingers slowly. I want you to come again for me, Elin, but only when I say." Marissa could hear the slapping sounds of the wet fingers moving in and out. "That's my girl. Can you feel me inside?"

"Y…yes. Now, I need to come now," Elin cried.

"Not yet, baby." She heard Elin's moans and felt her own need grow to a fever pitch. When she felt unable to wait, she commanded, "Now. Come for me now."

"Oh ahhhhhhh, oh god," Elin screamed. Marissa could imagine how the tremble started deep inside, causing the girl to lose all sight of space and time, concentrating only on the storm about to erupt in her body. "Oh, Marissa." Her own body was shattered with one tremendous orgasm.

"I love you so much. I need to see you and be with you."

"Impossible."

"Why?"

"Because it's over."

"No, it can't be," Elin said in a shaky voice.

"It is."

"You told me you loved and needed me. You said we have a connection."

"That was last weekend."

"No, I don't believe you."

"Believe it." Marissa hung up.

Marissa pulled her fingers out, lifted her hand, and looked at her still saturated fingers. She could still feel the fringes of her orgasm as she closed her eyes.

"Ah, sweet young, Elin, you were such a good fuck." She looked out her window at the rain. *I hate the rain.* She sighed heavily. "Unfortunately for you, dear Elin, I'm not the forever type."

†

Elin just held the phone as she heard the dial tone. "It can't be true. I know she loves me." She decided what to do and grabbed her purse, unlocked the door, walked out into the rain, relocked the door, and hailed a taxi.

"Fifty-fourth and Park," she told the cabbie.

When she got out of the cab, Elin looked up at the clock on the building with the rain pounding in her eyes. It was five thirty and somewhere inside was Marissa Banks. She would wait right there until Marissa either came out or went in. She needed to look into her eyes to know if what she had said was the truth or not.

Marissa exited the building at six thirty and raised her umbrella. She was in a foul mood and the rain wasn't helping. She felt the eyes upon her before she saw the young girl standing there in the rain. Even through the rain, she could see the salty wetness glistening on the smooth, young, and very pale skin. Instinct took over and she began to walk away until, for some unknown reason, she turned and looked back.

There was Elin, with her hand to her mouth, spastically coughing and bent over while catching herself from falling by grabbing onto a lamp post. *Shit.* Being a banker meant leaving no loose ends and Elin was unraveling her neatly tied rope. Next time she'd have to be more careful and not let them know where she worked. Marissa walked quickly to Elin. She positioned her umbrella over the small body so she had some cover from the rain. Marcus obviously did not get the message across to Elin clearly. He would be unemployed come Monday.

"What are you doing, standing in the rain without a coat?" she growled.

Elin just leaned into her and sobbed uncontrollably.

"This is getting tiresome. I've got better things to do. Straighten yourself up." Marissa raised her hand to hail a cab while pulling Elin closer under the umbrella. The girl was soaking wet and shivering, but fortunately, the sobs subsided when she put an arm around her. It wouldn't do to have her causing a scene in front of her workplace. She'd get the girl home and that would be that.

A cab stopped. "Come on, Elin, get in the cab. I'll take you home."

Marissa helped Elin slide into the backseat before she got in next to her. Elin put her head on her shoulder and it wasn't long before she heard Elin snoring softly.

"Where to, lady? I ain't got all day."

"Elin, what's your address?" When the girl didn't respond. Marissa fumbled in her briefcase until she came up with Elin's business card with her address scribbled on the back. She handed it to the cabbie. "Here's the address."

"The village at this time of day...this is gonna cost you."

"I don't care, just get us there." This scenario wasn't in Marissa's plans. To her, pity for others was a waste of time. She looked at Elin and felt a shiver go up her spine. "Do you have any idea just how much trouble you're causing me?" she whispered.

When the cab pulled up in front of Elin's building, Marissa shook her. "Come on, Elin, we need to get you inside."

Marissa helped Elin as she stumbled out of the cab. As they climbed the stairs and went inside, she let Elin lean against her. When they were outside of the door, Marissa watched as Elin's shaky hand tried to put the key in the lock.

Marissa snatched the key, jammed it into the door, twisted it, and then opened the door. "Let's go," she growled. "I haven't got time for your games." She put her hand on Elin's back and gave her a slight shove into the apartment.

"What are you doing to her?" Mrs. Wilkerson voice demanded.

Marissa turned and saw an older woman with her hands on her hips and suspicion in her eyes. "Mrs. Wilkerson? I am Marissa, Elin's friend. She's sick and I am helping her." She couldn't believe the nerve of the old bat to question her motives.

Mrs. Wilkerson gave Marissa a once over. "Humph. You better get her inside before she catches her death. She doesn't look so good."

Marissa smiled insincerely then pushed the door farther open. Once inside she said, "Get those wet clothes off so you can get in a hot shower."

"You take them off for me," Elin said. "I know how you like to do that."

Marissa angrily shook her head before she began undressing Elin and leading her into the bathroom and the shower. After what seemed to Marissa an intolerable length of time, Elin finally climbed into her bed and seemed to pass out. "Finally, I can get out of here."

Just as she was about to leave, Elin's thrashing in the bed became more and more violent. She pressed her hands on the girl's shoulder to try to stop her from hurting herself but was unsuccessful. Elin was sweating profusely, and her body seemed to Marissa to be burning up.

"Damn, she's really sick. Shit, I don't need this now. I should just leave her…it's not like I made her stand in the rain." She finally managed to get Elin to settle down, but she was still not doing so well. Marissa took out her phone, found a number, and pressed.

"Hey, it's me."

"Marissa, I can't come over tonight," the voice on the phone said.

"I need medical help."

"Are you ill?"

"No, it's someone else and I need you to look at her right now."

"What are the symptoms?"

"She is flailing around and has a high fever."

"Just give her some aspirin and lots of fluids. She should be fine in the morning."

"I don't think you heard me, Aimee. I said I want you to look at her now."

"I'll be over to your place shortly."

Marissa blew out a breath. "I thought you'd see it my way. I'm in Tribeca—"

"Tribeca? Are you slumming? I've never known you to be anywhere but in your hotel suite."

The comment didn't amuse Marissa.

"Just get here and bring your medical bag. The address is 1255 Barrelage, apartment B3."

Thirty minutes later, Marissa heard the buzz telling her that someone was at the main entrance. She pressed the button to unlock the apartment building door.

"It's about time you got here," Marissa barked as Aimee Sullivan entered Elin's apartment. Marissa walked briskly into the bedroom. "She's in here."

"Another one of your conquests?" Aimee asked as she entered the room. Once she saw Elin she gasped. "My, God, Marissa, how young is she?"

"Young, sweet, firm, and so delicious," Marissa replied. Her blue eyes darkened and bored into the doctor. "You know, I'm really not interested in what you think. You're here to make her better, so get busy."

Aimee shrugged, sat down on the bed next to Elin, and felt the girl's forehead before opening her medical bag.

"Well? Can you fix her? I've got things to do and can't spend my time playing nursemaid."

"Why are you here?" Aimee continued examining the girl.

"Why am I here? Isn't it obvious?"

"Not really. Your MO is to love 'em and leave 'em without a look backward. I think you once told me you take no prisoners."

"Look, she was standing in the rain and I thought she might die if I didn't get her warm and dry."

"And that matters to you? Right." The doctor laughed sarcastically. She put her stethoscope back in her bag. "Well, the good news for you is she will live."

"Can you get her to settle down so I can get out of here?"

"Ever the compassionate heart." Aimee frowned, wondering for the umpteenth time why she continued to let Marissa into her life. "Like I said, Marissa, she needs aspirin and fluids."

"Can you fix her?" Marissa's face was dark and angry.

Aimee focused her eyes on the person lying in the bed. "Her lungs are clear, and her temp is only slightly higher than normal. I suspect she is suffering from exhaustion and heartache." Aimee pulled the covers up around Elin's shoulders, before looking at Marissa again. "You know one of these days your games are going to come back and bite you in the ass. I gave her a mild sedative, so she should sleep through the night. I'll come back Sunday and check on her."

Aimee gathered her bag, stood, and started out of the room.

Marissa grabbed the doctor's wrist. "Not yet." Marissa's voice was low and laced with want.

Aimee looked over at the sleeping girl. "What about her?"

"I'm not interested in her." Marissa pulled Aimee close and kissed her hard as her hands caressed a firm backside.

Marissa knew Aimee would be helpless to resist and the doctor dissolved into her kiss. With urgency she kissed Aimee all the way to the couch where she had her way.

Later, as she left the apartment, Marissa took one last look and sighed before closing the door. The shop girl was very dangerous indeed and she was someone Marissa needed to get out of her life sooner rather than later.

CHAPTER TEN

Elin didn't know if it was a persistent tickle in the back of her throat or Kati that woke her, but she knew where she was. She looked at the clock on the bedside table—twelve thirty. By the light outside it was obviously afternoon. She couldn't remember the last time she had slept that late. A blurry memory that she couldn't quite bring into focus kept flashing in her mind. Then a brilliant smiled crossed her face as she remembered.

"Marissa," she whispered. "She brought me home." She looked around the room for her lover. "Marissa?" she called out, "Where are you?"

On wobbly legs, Elin got up and went in search of Marissa. She found her clothes piled in a heap on the bathroom floor. When she saw Kati's bowl empty, she felt a pang of guilt for neglecting her cat. After taking a can of cat food from the cupboard, she opened it and scraped the contents into Kati's bowl.

"There you go, sweetheart, I'm sorry." She brushed her hand across Kati's head. She continued her search only to have her heart sink when she realized that Marissa was no longer there. The events of the night before were foggy but one thing Elin knew was true: Marissa had been there. That alone gave her hope that Marissa's words "it's over" were meaningless.

Elin felt faint and held the kitchen counter in a tight grip. After steadying herself she finally realized just how her actions of the last week were affecting her health. Exhaustion was the first thought that came to her mind. For most of the week, she hadn't eaten, she just hadn't been hungry, and sleeping had been elusive. Mixed, they had left her feeling weak.

In the bathroom she rummaged through the medicine cabinet until she found the cold medication. She checked the expiration date and found the medicine had expired six months earlier. Nevertheless, she took a double dose before going back to bed. All she needed was to sleep some more and then she would be able to think clearly.

"Marissa loves me I know that."

She crawled under the covers, curled up in a fetal position, and covered her head with the blankets. "Marissa, where are you?" she whispered before she closed her eyes and fell into a deep sleep.

The insistent ringing of the phone woke her several hours later.

"Hello," she said groggily. "Mom? Why are you calling now?" She looked at the bedside clock again—three fifteen.

"Elin, darling, are you okay? You sound terrible." There was a long silence. "We need to talk about what's going on with you."

"Listen, Mom, I really don't feel very well, and I really don't want to go into who I sleep with. I'm old enough to make my own decisions." Elin feared that Marissa might try to call her and was anxious to end the call.

"I understand, Elin. Right now, I'm worried about you. You sound like you are coming down with something. Is there anything I can do for you? Do you want me to come down there?"

"No, Mom. It's nothing that a day or two in bed won't cure. That's why they have weekends," she said in a surly tone. "I'm sorry. I'll call you later in the week, okay?"

"All right, darling, please let me know if you want me to come and take care of you."

"I will." Once she ended the call, she turned her phone back on and dialed her own number to make sure that it still worked. Once out of bed, she moved around the rooms trying to find any evidence of Marissa's presence. She found none. She watched the street from the window in hopes of seeing Marissa walking toward her building or getting out of a cab. She never came. As darkness filled the sky, Elin finally left her station by the window and checked the phone for the tenth time. Still working.

"Where are you, Marissa?" An overwhelming sense of loneliness filled her heart as she swiped her fingers across her face to eradicate the moisture trickling down her cheeks. Was Marissa only a specter that built a nest inside her heart only to leave it empty? Her eyes began to burn once again. Then, somewhere between the truth of Marissa's words—"it's over"—and the pain invading her heart, she realized that

Marissa was gone, and she was alone. When tears fell unabated, she knew that nothing would ever be the same again and that her life was over. Going into her bedroom, she fell on the bed and began sobbing uncontrollably.

†

Elin pulled the covers over her head when she heard the soft mewing. "Kati, go away." She instantly felt bad. Kati gazed at her in what Elin thought was compassion. "I'm sorry I was angry with you. It's not your fault." She reached for the cat and gently stroked the soft fur. "Come on, let's get you something to eat."

After getting out of bed and going to the bathroom, Elin went to the kitchen, poured some dry food in the cat's bowl, then measured out coffee and started it dripping. Her eyes stung from the nightlong crying session. She tapped her fingers on the counter, waiting for her cup to fill with coffee. As she heard the final gurgling of the machine, a buzz sounded—someone wanted to enter the building.

"Marissa." She hurried to the intercom. "Yes," she said into the horizontal lines on the wall.

"It's Aimee. May I come up and see you?"

Aimee? "I think you must have pressed the wrong apartment's button. I don't know anyone named Aimee."

"I know Marissa."

Elin punched the button to allow entry. The simple mention of Marissa's name sent feelings of pleasure throughout her body. When she opened the door, she was amazed to see a casually dressed woman standing there with a medical bag in her hand.

"Is Marissa all right?" Elin focused on the bag and felt fear grip her heart.

"She's fine, I came to see you. Do you remember me from the other night?" The stranger's eyes followed Elin's stare. "It's my medical bag."

"Where are my manners? Please come inside...um...Doctor..." Elin was confused.

"Sullivan."

Once the doctor entered the apartment Elin closed the door.

"You say that you were here Friday night, Doctor Sullivan?"

"Yes, you were in a...shall we say...um...in a compromised state from standing in the rain."

"I don't get why I'd need a doctor?" Elin's eyebrows furrowed.

"Marissa thought you might be seriously ill and need medical help." The doctor cocked her head to the side. "She called me."

"I see." Elin could feel her face heat and she smiled brightly. "She was worried about me?"

"Yes, that is why she called me." The woman sounded frustrated.

"I just made some coffee, would you like a cup?"

"Yes, thank you. Black is good."

"Please take a seat and I'll be right back." Elin returned with two cups of coffee. "Here you go." She sipped her coffee, eyeing the doctor sitting on the couch.

"Have you been her friend for a long time?" Elin asked, afraid that the doctor was Marissa's lover or partner.

"Her friend? Marissa doesn't have friends. She only has conquests." Aimee scowled.

"I don't understand. If you're not her friend, why did you come when she asked you?"

"Why don't you sit over here next to me and let me examine you." Aimee patted the couch.

"If you're not her friend then what are you?" Elin sat down next to her.

Aimee took the stethoscope out of her ears.

"Are you her doctor?"

"No." The words seemed to be cautiously spoken. "I was involved with her just like you."

"Like me? I don't understand. Are you her partner?"

Aimee continued her examination. "Your chest sounds fine. How have you been sleeping?"

Elin rubbed the nape of her neck. "Except for Friday night I've been having some difficulty getting more than a few hours a night lately."

"What about your appetite? Are you eating regularly?"

"Not lately," Elin answered. "Please answer my question. Are you her partner?"

Aimee ignored the question. "Hmm, no appetite and sleepless nights that sounds familiar. I remember that happening to me a little over two years ago."

"I don't understand."

"Years ago, when I was on my family medicine rotation, I was her favorite for a weekend." She laughed derisively. "She breezed into my office and I had never met anyone like her. So charming and so sexy. That sensuous gaze of hers crawls under your skin and demands recognition. Somehow she bores a hole in your brain and fills it with thoughts of only her." Aimee gazed at Elin. "You know how that is, don't you? When out of nowhere this vision comes along and from that moment on it occupies your every waking moment."

Elin's hand instantly went over her ears as she began to understand what the doctor was trying to tell her. "I don't want to hear this. It is different for me."

Aimee smiled with compassion. "I thought that was the case too. I thought I would be the one to sweep *her* off her feet. It doesn't work that way for Marissa."

"No, you're lying. She loves me, I know it. Why else would she have brought me home the other night or called you to take care of me?"

"You don't get it do you?"

"Get what?" Elin cried out clutching her head.

"She didn't do all that for you, she did it for herself. It's always for and about her."

"No," Elin sobbed.

Aimee lifted Elin's chin. "Yes, unfortunately it's true. She'll use you until she's done with you and then she's gone."

"If all that is true then why did you help her out?" Elin sniffled. "Surely if she is as bad as you say you would have walked away from her." Elin's voice rose with righteous anger.

"I wish it were that easy. I've been trying ever since I was with her to do just that, but when she calls, I run to her."

"Why?"

Aimee shook her head and laughed. "Why indeed." For a moment, Aimee's eyes searched the room as she tried to find the right words. Elin deserved to know the truth no matter how much it might hurt her. When she had entered the apartment earlier and saw Elin's swollen, red-rimmed eyes, and haggard look, she knew the girl hadn't slept in days. Aimee's heart went out to Elin for she knew exactly what she was feeling. The doctor looked beyond Elin's outward appearance and saw something else—a sweet innocence. Marissa certainly knew how to pick the most vulnerable women.

"Answer my question," Elin growled. "Tell me why you keep going back."

"Because I truly believe that she will finally realize I am the one." Aimee lifted one shoulder. "Hope springs eternal. After all this time you'd think I'd know better." She touched Elin's hand. "I know how you feel."

"No, you don't. How could you? You have no idea how I feel."

"Yes, I do," Aimee said. "I've been where you are now, and I can guarantee there is no forever where Marissa is concerned."

"No, you're wrong." Elin swiped at her tear-filled eyes.

"Elin, is your heart breaking more than you ever thought possible?" Aimee asked softly.

"Yes."

"Has anyone ever hurt you like this before?"

"No."

"If she walked through your door right now what would you do? Pummel her and throw her out?"

"I couldn't do that to her."

"If she called you on the phone and said, 'I want to meet you' what would you do?"

"I'd go to her."

"Why?"

Aimee saw the dawning of the realization on Elin's face. She was finally beginning to understand what Aimee was telling her. Marissa was in Elin's blood and there was no way to eradicate her.

"She was my first. I thought it would be forever."

Empathy for Elin welled in Aimee's heart for she knew exactly how she felt. Aimee put her arm around the young woman and pulled her close.

"Forever for Marissa is from Friday evening to Sunday afternoon at the most. Some don't even get that. Oh, she will call you occasionally, and you will go to her because you can't help yourself. You tell yourself that this time will be different and this time she will stay. The sad truth, Elin, is that she never does."

"No, I won't go to her. I will never let her in again."

"Yes, you will."

Elin began to sob again uncontrollably for she knew the truth in those words. To Marissa she was nothing but a diversion. To her, Marissa was everything and she would do whatever was necessary to keep Marissa in her life.

Aimee fished in her bag, took out a business card, scribbled a number on the back and handed it to Elin. "If you ever want to talk or just have a shoulder to cry on call me. If you call the hospital, they won't let you talk to me, so I put my cell number on the back. I check those messages every hour."

Elin took the card and turned it over. "I called her every day and she never was available so why would you be."

"I promise I *will* call you back," Aimee said. "Everyone isn't like Marissa."

118

"Thank you," Elin held up the card, "for everything."

Aimee gently rubbed her thumb across Elin's cheek. She cocked her head and smiled.

"I have an idea if you're open to it."

"What is it?" Elin asked.

"Would you like to have dinner with me?"

Elin pulled away.

"I'm not ready for another relationship. This one has done all the damage I ever want to feel."

"No, you misunderstand—it's not a date. We can talk about what we feel and maybe come up with a plan for not letting it happen again," Aimee offered. "Let's just say it will be our way of eradicating Marissa from our lives." Aimee laughed. "Our own twelve step program."

"Hmm, that could have some merits." Elin straightened and wiped the last of the tears she vowed would never fall again for Marissa away.

"Yep, we can be each other's support system. If Marissa ever tempts us again, we will just be a call away to help the other say *no*. What do you say? Do you want to give it a try?"

"I'd like that. It will be good to have someone that understands to talk to about this."

"You know, we could be at this for a very long time. Even forever. Look at me," she touched her chest, "I've been under her spell for seven years."

Elin, for the first time, really looked at Aimee. She was very attractive and Elin guessed she was around ten years older than her. "I've got the time. Do you?"

"Yes." Aimee held out her hand. "Partners."

"Partners." Elin took the warm hand in hers and shook it.

"Good." Aimee drank the last of her coffee. "Let me get going. I have a few patients in the hospital to visit and then I'll go home and change." She looked at her watch. "What do you say I pick you up around five?" Her eyes searched Elin's. "Do you think you can be ready by then?"

"Will you really come back?" Fear gripped Elin.

Aimee patted her hand. "I'm not Marissa and yes, I will be back."

"Then I'll be ready."

Kati picked that moment to jump on Elin's lap and she smiled. "Aimee, this is Kati."

"Hi there, beautiful." Aimee placed a gentle hand on Kati's head and smiled. Her eyes found Elin's. "I have a cat too. Maxine is her name. Maybe they can have a play date sometime."

Elin smiled at Aimee's passing comment. "Maybe they can."

CHAPTER ELEVEN

Elin threw an outfit she'd just taken off onto the bed, and then rummaged through her closet for something else to wear when she went with Aimee to dinner. A brief smile curled her lips before the image of Marissa changed it to a frown.

"How could I have been so foolish that I'd believe her words? Obviously, they were all lies." Angry with herself she finally settled on a pair of skinny jeans, a button-down shirt, and boots. It wasn't a date, so she didn't need to go all out in the way she dressed. She had no idea of where they would be going but most places in the area had a laid-back way about them.

Apprehension filled Elin as five o'clock drew near. A small part of her hoped Aimee would arrive, but the biggest part—the unconfident part—knew she wouldn't. The buzzing coming from the intercom startled her and she paused before pressing the button. Only a few moments passed before there was a soft knock on the door.

"Hi, you came," Elin said when she saw Aimee.

"I said I would, and I always keep my word." She smiled. "Are you ready to go?"

"I'm sorry I don't have many visitors…would you like to come in and have a glass of wine? I think I have some Pinot Noir…maybe some white…"

Aimee chuckled. "Yes, I will join you for a glass of wine while we are having dinner."

"Oh, right." Elin shook her head. "Like I said, I don't go out very often. Where are we going?"

"I thought we'd go to one of my favorite hangouts, Glitter. It is within walking distance…it's just two blocks down the street and they have fantastic burgers."

Elin could feel her stomach clench and she drew in a breath.

"Is that a problem?" Aimee asked with concern in her voice. "We can go somewhere else if you like."

"No. No, Glitter is fine," she lifted a shoulder, "I was just surprised that's all…I didn't know you knew my neighborhood, that's all."

"I did my residency at New York Presbyterian Hospital, so I do know the area quite well. In fact, my apartment at the time was about a half mile from here."

"Where do you work now?" Elin asked with a smile.

"Columbia Hospital." Aimee gestured to the door. "Shall we go?"

"Sure." With apprehension, Elin locked the door and followed Aimee down the stairs. Her biggest fear now was running into the woman who had harassed her the last time she was at Glitter.

†

Elin could hear the laughter and music as she approached the door of Glitter with Aimee. She steeled herself for what was to come. Other than going out with the women from work, she could count on one hand the number of times she went out otherwise. When they walked inside Elin began searching the crowd to see if she saw anyone she recognized. *What was her name? Ah, yes, Chris. God, I hope she isn't here tonight.*

"Come on," Aimee said before grabbing Elin's hand.

They weaved in and out of groups of women until they came to an opening that had a beaded door. Aimee pushed on through.

"What is this place? Is this some sort of—" Elin stopped and gave Aimee a suspicious look.

Aimee held up her hand. "I'm not playing some sort of game if that is what you are thinking. I'm friends with the owner, Kathy, and this is a special area she set up for her friends that wanted to be out of the crowds. It will be quieter here and we can talk in private."

After she looked around the room that had three tables, one of which had a couple sitting there, Elin let her shoulders relax. "Like I said before, I have no reference for this."

"I know," Aimee said softly. "I'm not Marissa and I'll never play games with your emotions."

Elin listened to Aimee's words and realized that the doctor was asking her to trust her when Elin had no reason to. The earlier conversation she overheard between Aimee

123

and what seemed to be a distraught patient on the phone made her realize she did have a reason to trust. Aimee was a kind and decent person who probably didn't play games.

"Elin? I have no agenda here. Do you believe that?"

"To be honest, Aimee, I don't know you well enough to believe you. But from what I know about you so far, I would lean toward believing you."

"Good, that's a start." Aimee smiled. "What do you say we take that table over there in the corner?"

Once they placed their orders for burgers, fries, and beer, the two women sat in silence, each lost in their own worlds.

"You said it has been seven years since you met her, Aimee."

"Yes, that's true."

"Do you think you will ever be over her?"

"I think I am on that road now."

"I mean really over her, Aimee. To the point that if she calls you don't answer." Elin gave her an intense stare.

"I don't know. With everything that I am I hope so." Aimee shrugged. "What about you?"

"It's still too raw to make a judgement either way." She took a long drink of beer. "The intensity of what she made me feel isn't fading despite what I know now."

"She will try to suck you in again, Elin. You know that, don't you?"

"You're probably right, but she hasn't tried that yet so I really don't know. What I do know is that if she called, I'd go to her and—"

"Well, well look who we've got here...the tease."

Elin looked up at the speaker and saw who she remembered as the woman trying to get her into bed. "Please leave."

"You think she's going to put out but don't be fooled. She will lead you on and then leave you hanging." Chris stared at Aimee and then sneered. "I'd suggest you dump this one."

"I believe the lady asked you to leave." Aimee scooted her chair back and stood.

"What are you? Whipped?" Chris let out a maniacal sounding laugh.

Elin placed her hand on Aimee's arm. "Leave it. I'm sure she's not worth the effort."

Just then a woman dressed in jeans and a plaid shirt came into the room and stood by the table.

"Is this one giving you trouble, Doc?"

"No, she was just stopping by to say hello," Aimee said.

"Uh-huh. Not to doubt you, Doc, but I've dealt with her before." Kathy looked at Chris. "I told you the last time you made trouble for my customers, Chris, that I'd run you out of here and not let you back in."

"I didn't do nothing." Chris pointed at Aimee. "She told you I was just sayin' hi to my friend here."

"We both know that is a lie. Get out and don't come back," Kathy growled. Once Chris walked away, she said, "Sorry about that. She's a real troublemaker and it's about time I banned her."

"Thank you. Kathy, this is my friend Elin Prescot. Elin, this is Kathy Martinez...she owns the place."

Kathy held out her hand. "Pleased to meet you. Is this your first time here?"

"Um, no, I've been in here a few times." Elin could feel her cheeks heat up. "That's how Chris knows me..." She looked away.

"Hey, no worries. You are not the first one she's accosted. She thinks that sweet talk will get her into someone's pants and then gets pissed off when they reject her advances."

"Thank you for letting me know that," Elin said just as their burgers arrived.

"Not a problem. Well, I'll leave you to it. Enjoy."

"Sorry I brought you here," Aimee said placing her hand on Elin's.

"Thank you for defending me." She picked up the burger and took a bite. "Oh, this is fantastic. It never occurred to me to wrap a burger in lettuce."

"I always have lettuce instead of bread when I can,"

"I will remember to do that...although I don't eat out often."

"Why not?" Aimee asked.

"All my life I've had my eye on a prize and have worked toward that end." Elin placed her burger back in the basket. "I love designing clothes...always have. When I'm not at work I spend the time creating different designs and concepts. One day I hope to have my own clothing line."

"That's ambitious. Do you work with fashion now?"

"Yes, at Boutique La René."

"That's impressive. Personally, I don't think I could afford to shop there."

"Me either." Elin could feel sadness envelope her. "That's where I met Marissa. She strolled into the shop like she owned the world...she was magnificent, and I remember the first time I was alone with her and I had to catch my breath more than once." She sighed heavily and stared at the table.

"I can relate," Aimee said.

"Do you love her?" Elin lifted her head and looked directly at Aimee.

"No. I was more 'in lust' than anything else. When I'd see that it was her calling me, my body was set on fire all at once. I wanted her and always told myself this time would be different but it never was." Aimee's hazel eyes fixed on Elin. "She's a user and taker who is only out for herself."

"She was so intense and solicitous…that isn't something that anyone can fake."

"Unless you have honed your skills to be that way. Don't you see that, Elin? If she was sincere would she have told her PA to screen her calls and tell you she wasn't there?"

"How do you know she did that?" Elin demanded.

"Because she did that to me."

"Can I get you anything else," the waitress asked.

"Want another beer," Aimee asked.

Elin looked at her watch surprised that it was only six-thirty. "Sure, if you're having one too."

"Two more." Aimee held up her empty glass. "Whatever you have on tap is good."

"So, Aimee, tell me about you. Why did you become a doctor?"

"Well, my mom was a nurse and I found it amazing when I went with her on 'take your kids to work' day. From that moment on I wanted to be a doctor."

"That is really interesting. When I was five and wanted my mother to buy more clothes for my Barbie doll, she showed me how to make my own."

For the next few hours Elin and Aimee talked about their lives, family, and what their lives were like.

Elin looked up at the Miller beer wall clock. "Can you believe that it is almost nine?"

"Really?" Aimee smiled. "As they say, time flies—"

"When you're having fun." Elin laughed. "Tomorrow is my early day and I haven't done the laundry yet or gone to the market for food. Those are my two must-dos for the weekend."

"You've been sick. Want me to write you a get out of work pass?"

"Are you serious?"

Aimee nodded. "Of course, I am. You were seriously sick two days ago. As your doctor, I suggest you take a day or two off, so you can recover and get back to full speed."

"I wish I could. Tomorrow I have one of our major customers coming in and I can't blow that off."

"Come on, let's go. I can help you out with your laundry."

"That's sweet but I can't ask you to do that."

"Sure, you can. You didn't ask, I offered. That's step one in our program to move on: let others help you."

"Okay, and just how can I help you?" Elin slid her chair back and shook her head.

"You already have."

"How?"

"By coming here with me. I was terrified, and you helped me overcome that."

"Why were you terrified?"

"The whole situation with Marissa...you and I meeting through her...I wasn't sure how this would all work out. That you'd judge me by her and think I am the same and I'm—"

"Hold on." Elin held up her hand palm out. "That is not who I am, Aimee. I look at you for who you are and that's all."

"Thank you."

"I was scared too. The last time I was here was when I had the run in with Chris. I thought for sure she was going to follow me home and take me by force...rape me." Elin chewed on her lip. "Ever since I didn't want to go out on my own."

"Then we helped each other for almost the same reason. Let's get going. I need to do my laundry so I have something to wear tomorrow, and stop at the market for a few things to have enough food for a few more days."

"Fair enough." Aimee took her hand. "Come on I'll walk you home."

"Do you have any plans for when you get home?" Elin asked.

"I think I will just go home and go to bed."

CHAPTER TWELVE

After Aimee saw her to the door of her apartment's building, and Elin did a little laundry, she fell into bed exhausted from the events of the weekend. She hadn't set the wake-up alarm and woke up ten minutes later than normal. Still she was able to get ready in time to catch the subway to work. Elin made it to work with ten minutes to spare.

"Good morning, Bess," Elin said as she entered Boutique La René. "How was your weekend?"

Bess turned and the smile she had faded. "Elin, what's wrong?"

"Nothing." Elin could see in her boss's eyes why she asked.

"You look like someone the dog drug in. Are you sick?" she asked with concern in her voice.

"I think I had a bit of the flu over the weekend but I'm better now."

"If this is better, I hate to think how you looked on Saturday. Did you see a doctor?"

"Yes."

"And?"

"She told me to take it easy for a few days and I did. Now I'm ready to work. We have our new client today and I have everything ready for her." Elin smiled. "I'm good...promise."

"Frankly, you look like you haven't slept in days." Bess shook her head. "As you know, Ms. Gerard is a high-profile client and she asked for you specifically. If you aren't one hundred percent, please let me know now so I can make arrangements."

"Have I ever failed to do my job for you or the boutique?" Elin watched as Bess slowly shook her head. "And, I won't this time. Please trust me on this."

She didn't know who she was trying to convince—Bess or herself. In the mirror that morning she could see how haggard she looked and had seriously considered calling in sick, but she knew how important the new client was and she wasn't going to let Bess down.

"Go reapply your make-up and hopefully that will help." Bess took off her glasses and rubbed her eyes.

"I will, Bess. Don't worry I won't mess this up."

†

Elin had no expectations of the new client, Holly Gerard. The CEO of a mega shopping conglomerate turned out to be affable and easy to work with. Like most of Elin's clients, the woman knew what she wanted and liked, and Elin had focused her selections in the direction of what she observed. Two hours later Elin was going through her notes when Bess tapped softly on the open door.

"Bess, come on in."

"Ms. Gerard seemed pleased when she left."

"She is delightful and was easy to work with. Not at all what I expected."

"Most of them are until they are dissatisfied, then watch out." Just then the store's phone rang. "I'd better get that."

Elin digested Bess's comment and thought of Marissa right away. The ache of her dismissal still bore heavily on her heart and she once again felt devasted.

"There's a call for you on line three, Elin," Bess said, poking her head in the door.

Marissa. With panic wrestling with hope she looked at Bess and held her breath.

"It's your doctor."

"Okay thank you, Bess." Elin could feel her heart deflate. She picked up the phone. "Hello, Doctor Sullivan."

"How are you feeling?"

"To be honest, not great."

"Is there any way you can go home and just take care of yourself?"

"I can't just leave work in the middle of the day." Elin looked up and saw Bess was still in the doorway and mouthing *Yes you can.*

"Why not?"

"I just can't just walk away. Can you understand that?"

"Of course I can. It would be like me leaving stitches half done."

"You get it then."

"Yes, I get it and you. Would you like me to bring you some soup later?" Elin could picture a smile on Aimee's face.

"Thanks, but no. I think I will go home and just relax...maybe I'll take a hot bath."

"Sounds good. Take care of yourself and if you get to feeling worse, please let me know."

"I will. Goodbye." Elin looked at Bess. "How did she know I was sick?"

"Don't know. She told me she was Dr. Sullivan and asked how you were looking and said she wanted to speak with you." Bess grinned. "I told her you looked like shit."

"Is it okay if I finish up here and then go home? To be honest I *do* feel like shit." She gave her boss a slight grin.

"Yes, and I want you to stay there until you are all better. That means take two or three days. Okay?"

"Yes, boss." Elin cleared up the account she was working on and then put on her coat and left the shop. When she stepped out onto the street she wasn't sure she'd make it to the subway so she hailed a taxi.

†

Elin trudged up the stairs to her apartment using the last bit of strength she had. On the cab ride home, her mind filled with thoughts of Marissa. How had she been so wrong about the woman? Sure, she hadn't any experience in even dating but she'd seen...what in Marissa's eyes...love? If she was truthful, she hadn't seen any sort of affection, only desire. Now, standing in her apartment with Kati rubbing up against her leg, she began to reflect on Aimee's words. "Marissa has no friends only conquests." Surely that was not all she was to Marissa.

"She sent me flowers. She made love to me," Elin whispered. Then in the deepest recesses of her soul she knew the truth and she fell to the floor and began to sob. By the time she struggled to her feet and looked out the front window, it was twilight. Kati who snuggled next to her meowed.

"I know, you're hungry." She dragged herself to the kitchen, opened the refrigerator door, took out a can of cat food, and fixed Kati's dish. Once Elin finished, she made her way to the bedroom where she dropped her clothes on the floor, got in bed, and cried some more before falling into a fitful sleep.

The next day Elin woke up disorientated as her eyes took in the brightly lit room. Something wasn't right. Her bedroom should be still dark just like it was most mornings she woke for work at this time of year. She looked at the clock radio on the table next to her bed. Eleven fifteen. She bolted straight up.

"I'm late for work. Damn it all to hell." Elin's eyes tracked to the pile of clothes on the floor and stopped. Bess had told her to take two days off. "Or was it three?"

After going to the bathroom, Elin flopped back on her bed and covered her eyes with her arm. How long had it been since she'd first met Marissa? A week? No. A month? Maybe. She really didn't know.

"How can I not know? She had a profound effect on me…she was my everything and I haven't a clue as to how long I've known her. No wonder she dumped me."

Over the next two days, Elin was in a lackluster mood but managed to get her laundry done and opted to call and have her groceries delivered. That was an expense she really couldn't afford but she had no desire to dress and go out. Her cell phone rang off and on over the days. She did listen to the messages from her mom, Bess, and Aimee, only bothering to return Aimee's calls. She knew if she didn't the doctor would come to her door and she wasn't in any mood for conversation. Each time her phone rang she hoped to hear Marissa's voice, worried about her. It never happened. Finally, on her last day of rest, she had a productive PJ day and let herself become lost in the designs that whirled in her mind, drowning out all thoughts of Marissa.

CHAPTER THIRTEEN

"Well don't you look much better," Bess commented when Elin walked into Boutique La René.

"Thank you for insisting I take some time off. I hadn't realized how run down I was." Elin smiled at her boss. "Now I'm ready to get back to work."

"Perfect. We have Mrs. Armstrong coming in at eleven and she requested you."

"Okay, I'll bring up her files and get ready for her." Elin turned to go to her office but turned back when Bess spoke again.

"What's in the portfolio?"

"Oh, I've been working on some designs and wanted to get your take on them if we get a chance today."

"Why don't we plan to have lunch together and you can show me then."

Elin could feel the first genuine smile she'd had in close to a week curve her lips. "I'd like that. Thank you again for letting me take time off."

"We all get to a point in life where we have to take a step back and recharge our batteries, Elin. If that ever happens again, you just tell me that you need some time and I will give it to you." Bess patted her arm and smiled. "I'm glad you're back. I missed seeing you."

"Me too." Elin's emotions were still raw enough that the kind words made her want to cry but she held back as she walked quickly to her office. Once inside with the door closed, she leaned back against it and took a deep cleansing breath and pulled herself together. At her desk she picked up Mrs. Armstrong's file, opened it, and began a search for the perfect garments for her.

Elin was just finishing updating the Armstrong files when Bess knocked on the doorframe, holding a bag in her hand. "How did it go?"

"Great. She is such a sweet lady. I told her that I thought everything looked good on her and she agreed." Elin got up from her chair. "Is it lunch time already?"

"I brought your favorite cob salad and an iced tea."

"Sounds yummy." Bess held up another sack and Elin grinned. "Is that what I think it is?"

"If you are thinking a triple chocolate brownie, you're wrong." Bess laughed. "Of course, that is what it is."

"Then why don't you come on in and we will have lunch." Elin rubbed her hands together.

"So, tell me how you are doing, Elin. I was worried about you," Bess said after they began eating their salads.

"Well…" Elin didn't want to lie about her breakdown over Marissa, so she chose her words carefully. "I think somehow my life got sideways and I tried too hard to get it straightened out. I ended up, as they say, 'burning the candle at both ends' and running my body into the ground." She looked up to judge if Bess was either accepting or not her explanation. A blank expression greeted her. "I wasn't eating or sleeping, and I got run down…at least that is what the doctor told me." Elin held her breath.

"You should have come to me." Bess reached over and covered Elin's hand with hers. "I was afraid for you because you looked so…what's the word…unreachable and lost. Each day you came in you looked worse than the day before. Why didn't you confide in me?"

"The truth?" Bess nodded for her to go on. "Because I had no idea that anything was wrong until Friday evening when my body finally let me in on the secret it was that worn out."

"Well then, in the future if I see you that way again, I will take action."

"Thank you. I would appreciate it."

"Now, are you going to show me your new designs?"

Glad for a change in subject, Elin took out her portfolio.

"I got the idea for this collection from working here. Why not have stylish work outfits for those who are not in power positions in a company and make them affordable."

"Okay, let's see what you have." Bess took her time and looked at each drawing. "I like that they aren't copies of what we sell but original designs. Take this one," she turned two pages and tapped the page, "it looks chic yet comfortable."

For the next hour they discussed the pros and cons of each design. When Bess finally left, Elin had ideas swirling about on how to refine her designs. For the first time since the debacle with Marissa, Elin could feel a surge of confidence and joy. After all this was her life's dream, and she now could see a light guiding her down that path. There was no way she'd let someone like Marissa Banks destroy the path she'd chosen.

†

Friday, Elin trudged up the stairs to her apartment, surprised at how exhausted she was after only working two days. At the same time, she could feel an upbeat mood taking hold as she remembered the time with Bess as they went over her designs. From early childhood, all Elin wanted to do was create a clothing line much like the one she made for her dolls. Bess's praise gave her the impetus to move forward and leave all thoughts of Marissa behind. The familiar jab to her heart happened just thinking of Marissa, but Elin resolved to push her out of her mind and concentrate on what was important.

After she opened the door, she locked it before kicking her heels off and wiggling her toes. She had two days ahead of her to work on her clothing line. The time off earlier in the week had helped her get ahead of the laundry, cleaning, and food shopping. Her phone rang, and she looked at the caller ID and was surprised to see Aimee's name.

"Hi," Elin said. "Is everything okay?"

"Yes. I was checking up on you to see how you are feeling after going back to work."

"To be honest, Aimee, while I was riding home on the subway, I felt like a truck ran over me, but as soon as I got home, I was tired but good. Does that make any sense at all?"

"It does. I bet the first thing you did was kick your shoes off."

"How did you know that?"

"Because that is what I do. My day consists of standing, walking, and sometimes running so getting those shoes off is delightful."

Elin could imagine the smile on her face from Aimee's voice. "Except for the running I know exactly what you mean. How was your day?" Elin sat in her favorite oversized chair and put her legs up on the ottoman.

"Actually, I had a pretty good day. I was going back to my office from a meeting and there was a very pregnant woman bent over about to deliver a baby. I helped with that until the OB on call came. Other than that, the day was routine."

"What was it?"

"The baby?"

"Yes."

"A girl. Little thing just barely five pounds."

"I've always admired doctors, nurses, and first responders because they make a difference in other's lives."

"Do you really think so? It is just a job."

"No, it is so much more than just a job. You are out on the front lines, diagnosing and helping people find comfort or peace." Quiet filled the air. "Are you still there, Aimee?"

"Yes. You humble me," she said softly. "Have you eaten yet?"

"No. I just got home."

"Want to have dinner with me?"

"As much as I'd like to say 'yes' I don't think I have the energy to get ready and put shoes on again."

"How about some Chinese take-out? I'll bring it to your door."

"Now that's an offer I can't refuse." Elin could feel the first genuine smile of her day curl her lips.

"Anything special you like?"

"Surprise me."

"Okay then. I'll probably be there within the hour, depending on how crowded Ming Chow's is."

"Great. Beer or wine?"

"Neither, I'd probably fall asleep on you."

"I'd be right there with you. See you soon." Elin laughed.

"Bye."

"Bye," Elin said before she disconnected the call, still smiling.

†

Forty-five minutes later, Elin heard a tap on her door and frowned. She hadn't heard the signal that someone wanted into the building. On her tiptoes she made her way quietly to the door and looked through the peep hole. Aimee. She flung the door open.

"You didn't beep first."

"There was a guy coming out, so I just came in." Aimee's eyes searched Elin's. "Did I scare you?"

"Just a little. Come on in." Elin pointed to the bag Aimee was holding. "That smells delicious."

"I hope you like my choices. I got shrimp lo mein, garlic chicken, egg rolls, and my favorite crab Rangoon."

"Have I gone to a Chinese restaurant with you?"

"No, I don't believe so." Aimee scrunched her forehead. "Why do you ask?"

"Because you got exactly what I'd get." Elin rubbed her hands together. "I'll get us plates. Are chopsticks good with you?"

"Definitely chopsticks." Aimee smiled. "Where should I put the bag?"

"How about on the coffee table. It will be easier to share that way."

Aimee put the bag down and stood in the small living room, looking at the pictures on the wall. "Are these your designs?" she asked.

"Yes, that was what I did for my final at Parsons. That design was the runner-up for the A' Design and Award Competition."

"I can see why. Is that what you want eventually…to be a designer?"

Elin smiled. "It's been a lifelong dream of mine."

"That's it for me. I don't think I can eat another bite." Aimee pushed her lo mein away and scooted back on the sofa.

"Me too. Thank you for this wonderful surprise. I probably would have settled for an almond butter sandwich." Elin leaned back against the couch and rubbed her stomach. "You said on the phone you were going to some restaurant I haven't heard of."

"Yes, Ming Chow's. I've been going there for years. When I was a struggling intern, I'd go there at least three times a week. They had generous portions for a reasonable price." Aimee laughed. "They now know me by name, and I think they always give me more than normal."

"I envy you," Elin said whimsically.

"Why?" Aimee gave her a quizzical look.

"I've lived in this apartment for almost five years, and other than the market or the basement to do laundry, the only place that I've been to more than once is Glitter. It was my third time when I went with you."

"Why haven't you gone out more? This is New York City and the opportunities to explore are almost endless."

Elin smiled and shook her head. "I take the crowded subway to and from work, and at the end of the day I've had enough of people jostling me. When the weekend rolls around I just want to veg."

"So, it's a good bet that you've never been to the Guggenheim?"

"The museum?" Elin asked.

"Yes."

"I haven't been there. Too daunting for me to go alone."

"There is a special showing of the masters this weekend that I was going to go to. Would you like to come along?"

Elin looked into Aimee's eyes and only saw sincerity. "Well, I'd—"

Aimee's phone rang, she looked at the caller ID, and her eyes went wide. "It's Marissa. I'll put it on speaker." She looked at Elin. "Okay?"

Elin nodded.

"Hello."

"Hey, baby, I'm lonely and want you."

When Elin heard the silky voice, she could feel her body react with want and need.

"Not interested," Aimee said in a tight voice.

"You know you are, darling, so stop whatever you are doing and get over here."

Elin wanted to put her coat on and rush to Marissa's side but realized that it wasn't her call but Aimee's. *Why doesn't she want me?* Then she looked at Aimee and felt ashamed of her thoughts.

"Marissa, after what I saw you do to that girl, I'm done with you. You just don't treat people like that."

"She got what she deserved. No one comes to my office building unless I ask them to and that crazed girl wouldn't take a hint. You get over here now," Marissa growled.

"No. Go find yourself someone else, Marissa, I'm done with you." Aimee ended the call and looked at Elin. "Are you okay?"

Elin shook her head.

"What you heard is the real Marissa Banks and not the sweet-talker you thought she was. I'm sorry you had to hear that." Aimee put her arm around Elin's shoulders and pulled her close.

Elin let out a long sigh as her heart once again broke. She now realized that what Aimee told her was true and Marissa was nothing more than a taker.

"Don't spend the weekend here alone stewing over that hateful woman. Come with me to the museum. What do you say?"

"I'd like that."

For the next hour Aimee held Elin as she quietly sobbed.

CHAPTER FOURTEEN

Elin lounged in bed Sunday morning recalling her visit to the Guggenheim with Aimee. She had been familiar with photographs and reproductions of great artists' works, from Van Gogh to Picasso, but they paled when compared to the real thing. She had never really appreciated art until the day before, and now she considered what all the other museums of New York City had to offer. Her family home was about an hour away in Stamford, Connecticut, yet they had never come to New York to sightsee. They had gone on trips all over the United States and Canada, but her father had said that there was too much crime in the city to visit. In the five years she'd lived there, crime had never visited her, except for the altercation with Chris at Glitter. Now, thanks to Aimee, a whole new world had opened to her.

It was nine twenty and in a few minutes her mother would call, as she did every Sunday since Elin had moved away from home. She had always looked forward to the calls for they made her feel safe and warm. Except now. Ever since she told her mother that she spent the night in a same sex relationship, their conversations had become stilted and awkward. Elin's mind recalled the weekend she'd spent with Marissa. Could that have only been two weeks ago? It seemed longer. All she knew was the deep, all-consuming loss that she felt. How she needed her mother and the understanding she always brought whenever Elin had a problem. Now that would not happen, and she wondered if it ever would again. Her cell phone rang, and she answered.

"Hi, Mom, how are you and dad doing today?"

"We are getting ready to go to Mass. Your dad has a bit of a cold, so we won't go out to brunch with the church group."

"Is he drinking lots of fluids and taking vitamin C?"

"Yes, he is. How are you feeling?"

"Much better." Elin wanted to cry *please help me, Mom, I'm so confused,* but she didn't.

"Maybe you could come home one weekend."

"Mom, I don't know when I can get away. We are very busy at work." Elin wasn't lying but, at the same time, she knew that Bess would let her take some time off to visit her parents.

"I'll make you all your favorites. It's been a while since I've been able to take care of my little girl."

Elin could hear the sincerity and hope in her mother's voice. She looked at the clock and knew that any moment her mother would have to go. Desperate for her mother's comfort she said, "Mom, I'll try to see what I can do."

"That will be wonderful, Sunny."

Elin sucked in a breath and closed her eyes when she heard her mother's nickname for her. Her mind flashed to her mother singing 'You Are My Sunshine' to her at bedtime.

"Well it is time for us to leave, your dad is at the door. Take care of yourself. I will light a candle for you. Come and see us soon, we miss seeing you."

"As soon as things calm down I will, Mom."

"Great. Goodbye."

"Bye, Mom." Elin ended the call knowing that all she gave were excuses as why she didn't visit more and began to softly cry. What she wanted was to go to her mother and feel soothed, but she didn't want to reveal what a fool she'd been. She'd allowed her life to take an unexpected turn by allowing Marissa Banks to dupe her. Yet, she couldn't deny the need to be with Marissa on any level she would have her. Elin curled up in a ball and wept until she fell into a fitful sleep.

†

On Friday evening Elin merged onto Highway 95 toward her parents' home in Connecticut. It usually took about an hour and twenty minutes depending on the traffic. Friday afternoon was the beginning of the weekend and Elin knew it would take longer. She really didn't mind since the extra time would give her a chance to settle her thoughts. It had been a hectic week at the shop with everyone wanting new outfits for the upcoming summer. Over the five days she had seen two clients each day, and when she saw the last one out the door, Elin drew in a deep breath.

"I thought this week would never end," Elin said to Bess.

147

"Me either but the commissions we get will be worth it." Bess patted her arm. "Are you ready for your trip?"

"Yep, I have a bag and the rental car is full of gas, so as soon as I straighten my things, I'll be off. I am hoping to beat the traffic."

"I'll tidy things for you." Bess put her arm around Elin's shoulders and gave her a little squeeze. "I'm glad you are taking this trip. I was so worried about you a few weeks ago, I thought we might lose you."

Elin leaned into her boss. "Thank you for everything. I don't think I'd have made it without your support."

"Well, you did have your doctor too. Each time she called I could hear the genuine concern in her voice."

"Yes, Doctor Sullivan is an excellent doctor. She called here?" Elin asked confused by the comment.

"Well, yes she did. At first, when she called for your phone number, I asked if she'd keep me informed on how you were doing, and she did."

"Oh. She never told me that." Elin looked at her watch. "I will take you up on your offer and go ahead and get on the road."

"Have a great time, dear. I'll see you on Monday."

"Okay, thanks." Elin smiled and left the building.

†

"Sunny, you're here." Dorothy Prescot engulfed her daughter in a tight hug. She took a step back and held Elin at arm's length. "You are a sight for sore eyes. I can't believe you're here."

Elin smiled and looked over her mother's shoulder to her father who was wiping at his eyes. This certainly wasn't the greeting she was expecting but she'd take it.

"I'm glad to be here." She moved away from her mother to hug her dad. "Daddy, it's good to see you."

"You too. How was the traffic?"

"Not bad considering it is a Friday night. It only took a little over an hour and a half."

"You made good time then." He gave her another hug and then let go.

"Come on in the house, everyone is here," Dorothy said before wrapping an arm around Elin's shoulders.

Elin could feel her stomach roil as she wondered if they all knew about her tryst with a woman.

"Everyone," she asked, "who would that be?" She really wasn't up for a big family reunion after working all day before driving to get there.

"No worries, Sunny, it is just your brother and sister. Tomorrow your grandparents are coming around for dinner."

"Sunny, you're home. I've missed you so much." Patty, Elin's sister, pulled her into a hug.

"I missed you too, Sis. How is school going?"

"Great. I got accepted at Ryder."

"Fantastic. I've heard great things about that school. You will like it there. Where's Robby?" Elin looked around the room.

"I'm right here, sis. Wanna beer?"

"This is so wonderful," Dorothy said. "All my kids together in the same room. It's been a long time since that happened. Come on, supper is ready. I made your favorite, Sunny, pot roast."

Elin smiled and let her shoulders relax. She was home, and everything seemed to be the same as it always had been. Her mom was rushing around cooking to please everyone. Her dad stood by with a quiet and reserved strength. Patty was bubbly and bouncy, bringing sunlight to all around her, and Robbie was the older brother who always stood up for her. All her apprehension was gone and the warmth of being with family filled her.

†

Saturday afternoon found Elin sitting at the kitchen table having coffee with her mother. Her dad and Robby were out in the garage working on an old GTO that they were restoring. Patty had left to go shopping with her friends.

"It's quiet," Dorothy said. "I don't get many of those days." She took Elin's hand and squeezed it. "Tell me about this woman you're in love with."

Elin pulled her hand away. "There's nothing to tell. It's over."

"Oh, sweetheart, what happened?"

"She duped me into thinking she cared...took what she wanted and then never spoke to me again. I made such a fool of myself, Mom, and I don't know what to do." Tears began to fall slowly but soon they were streaming down her cheeks. "No matter how hard I try to forget, Mom, I still feel the pain here." Elin placed a hand over her heart.

"It will be okay, Sunny. I promise that someone else will come along who is so much more than that...that floozie."

Elin laughed.

"What's so funny?"

"Mom, if you met her you wouldn't call her that." Elin closed her eyes. "Why doesn't she want me?"

Dorothy pulled Elin to her and held her close. "Don't waste your tears on someone who won't ever appreciate them. She's not worth it."

"I don't know if I can trust anyone again. It hurts so bad."

Dorothy continued to hold her daughter close, whispering words of support and love.

Elin finally lifted her head and swiped her hand across her cheek and nose.

"Here." Dorothy handed her a tissue.

"Thanks. I don't know why I'm blubbering so much. It seems like I do it all the time and can't stop."

"Do you have someone to talk to?"

"Yes. Aimee. She was a castoff too." Elin let a small smile curve her lips. "We've formed a support group of two."

"I'm glad you have that." Dorothy pulled away and looked directly at Elin. "Have you always been attracted to women or just this one?"

It finally came. The question Elin had been waiting for. She knew her mother had made sure everyone was gone so they could have this talk about whom she slept with in private. Elin nodded.

"I take that as a yes," Dorothy said softly.

"Mom, we are having a nice visit, please don't do this."

"Do what?" Dorothy looked confused.

"Tell me how awful I am for loving women, and that I'm going to go to hell if I don't go to confession and beg for forgiveness. I won't do it. There is nothing to forgive," Elin growled through clenched jaws.

"Sunny, sweetheart, I wasn't going to say anything like that. You told me on the phone that you choose the person and not the gender, and I thought and prayed about that. I realized that is the only way to judge people—by who they are not who they love." Dorothy reached out and swiped her thumb across the tear-stained cheek of her daughter. "I love you unconditionally, Sunny. I always have and always will. You are my sunshine and that will never change."

"What about Dad? Does he think that way too?"

"He told me he loved you no matter what."

"I love you too, Mom. Thank you for everything." Elin began to cry again. This time not from a broken heart but for her lack in the faith of her parents' love.

"Come on, let's get supper ready. Your grandparents always come early expecting to eat right away."

"What do you need me to do?" Elin let out a little laugh and got up from her chair just as Patty came through the door. "We have another helper." Elin gave her sister a big grin.

"Come on, girls, we have a feast to prepare."

†

Late Sunday evening Elin finally arrived back in her apartment, exhausted but happier than she'd been in a while. Her phone rang, and she smiled before answering.

"Hi. I'm home safe and sound."

"I figured this would be about the time you'd get back. Did you have a good time?" Aimee asked hesitantly.

"Yes, I did. I had a long talk with my mother, came out to my brother and sister, and I'd call it a successful family-bonding time. Bottom line, they love me and that is what is most important."

"Yes, it is. I'm glad that it all worked out." There was a long pause.

"Aimee, are you still there?"

"Yes. I have to tell you something."

"Marissa"—just to say her name made Elin shiver—"called and you went to her," Elin whispered.

"Partially correct. She did call, and it took all that I had to tell her no, but I did."

"Do you think she will get the message and leave you alone?"

"Marissa is an egomaniac and a user. I doubt she will ever really get the message. Now that I've turned her down twice it will intensify, I'm afraid.

"Remember you have a support group of one and I am always here for you no matter the time or day. You should have called me when it happened."

"Nah, I wasn't going to ruin your weekend with her. She isn't worth it."

"She isn't...is she?" Elin closed her eyes and silently sighed.

"It's getting late. I'd better let you go. I'll talk with you later in the week. Good night, Elin."

"Good night, Aimee." Elin disconnected and let out a sob. Why hadn't Marissa called her? "I would have gone to her." She shook her head. "No, I can't think that way...I just can't." In her heart she knew that wasn't the truth.

CHAPTER FIFTEEN

Elin was in a subway car when her phone rang. She smiled. It was Aimee.

"Hey, what's going on?"

"Can you be ready by six?"

"For what?"

"I'm taking you out to dinner."

"Oh, you are, are you?"

"Yep. So, can you be ready?"

"Yes."

"Great see you then."

Elin ended the call and smiled. Aimee calling her out of the blue and wanting to take her some place or another had become normal, and it made Elin feel warm and happy. Her mind immediately went to what outfit she'd wear.

154

Once in her apartment she quickly changed her clothes before feeding Kati. When six fifteen rolled around Elin paced the floor and kept checking the time, looking out the window. It was unlike Aimee to be late without calling to tell her.

"Do you think she will actually show up tonight, Kati?" She looked at the clock again and sighed. Six twenty-five. Elin knew that she wasn't like Marissa and she worried that something had happened to Aimee.

The sound of the buzzer made Elin jump before she rushed to push the button. When she heard the soft tap on the door, she opened it.

"Hi."

"Hi yourself. Sorry I'm late. Just as I was walking out the door a man came stumbling in and I had to make sure he got to the right place. I tried to call but it went straight to voice mail."

"It did?" Elin pulled her phone out of her pocket and looked at the silence button. On. "Well, duh, I had it on no ring."

"No problem. Are you ready? I've got a cab waiting."

Elin smiled and grabbed her keys off the table by the door. "Yep, let's go." Elin followed the doctor down the stairs and into the cab.

"So where are we going?"

"A little Italian place in the east village. It's one of my favorites."

"Sounds great." Elin liked being with Aimee. She was fun and always had a smile on her face.

Aimee opened the door for Elin when they arrived at Little Italy. A gray-haired man greeted them.

"Ah, Doctor, it is good to see you again," he said in a thick Italian accent. "I have a nice table just for you."

Elin peered covertly over her menu at Aimee sitting across from her. "What do you recommend?"

"Anything on the menu is good, Elin. My personal favorite is the linguine with sausage, but I've had the rosemary chicken which is good, too."

After placing the food and drink order, Elin smiled.

"It's nice to be here with you."

"I have the same opinion." Aimee gave her a curious look. "Did your parents' name you after a family member? I have never seen 'Ellen' spelled like that."

"My great grandmother's name was Regina Elin Carlson. She emigrated here from Sweden and I am named after her. My mother always told me that Elin is the equivalent of Helen in the Scandinavian and Dutch languages." Elin grinned. "What about you, is there some hidden meaning to Aimee?"

Aimee laughed heartily. "First of all for the record, I like the name Elin. As for me, I was born with red hair and green eyes and my mother really wanted to name me Rita, but fortunately for me she didn't. I think I lucked out. Ah, here is our meal."

The waiter placed their plates in front of them. "Can I get you anything else?" he asked.

"No, everything looks delicious."

"*Mangio bene,*" he said before leaving the table.

Elin saw Aimee watch her as she took her first bite.

"This is fantastic. I love lasagna, and this is by far the best I've ever had." Elin twirled her fork in the air and sighed in satisfaction. "How did you ever find this place?"

"I used to live right down the street from here. The food is delicious and, best of all, the price was inexpensive, which was great for a struggling resident. In fact the Chinese we had before came from a place two streets over. I'm glad you like it."

"Did you always want to be an ER doctor?" Elin asked.

"Yes. I've always been interested in the workings of the body. I started in a practice with a group in uptown Manhattan but changed to one at the hospital."

For a long moment, they sat silent, each deep in thought.

"So how did Marissa really find you?" Aimee cocked her head.

"If she sees a woman she wants, she makes a plan on how to capture them."

"How do you know that?" Elin's forehead rose in question.

"She had no problem bragging to me about all her conquests. Sad to say, you were just another notch on her bedpost. Any idea where she saw you first?"

Elin scrunched her face in a frown and tried to find her voice.

"Oh, she didn't find me, it was more of an accident, she really came into the shop to work with Bess." She wiped a hand over her eyes. "I had never met anyone so charming and captivating."

Aimee reached across the table and touched Elin's hand. "Hey, remember we are in this together."

"Yeah, so tell me the story of how she found you? You said she came in for a physical, were you her doctor?"

"No, she found me. Not sure how. I don't recall ever seeing her before. She showed up in the clinic during my internship, demanding to have a physical exam and insisting that I was who she wanted for a physician." Aimee laughed. "Her presence alone makes things happen for her, so she got the appointment. I remember when I walked into the exam room and saw her it was…" her eyes rolled upwards as she tried to find the right words, "…damn, she took my breath away. I had never met or seen anyone so completely beguiling and I was instantly drawn to her." Aimee shook her head and laughed softly. "She managed to make the entire exam a sensual experience. When I listened to her heart, she took the stethoscope away and opened her gown telling me I could hear the beat clearer that way. Of course, when she did that it exposed her breasts and I had to fight to keep my eyes from them. I remember thinking she must hear my heart pounding." She shrugged.

"I was totally smitten, and I am sure she knew it. She insisted on a gynecological exam. I didn't need much lubricant and when I did the internal exam, I felt her contract around my fingers. By the end of the exam I couldn't think straight so when she bent in and kissed me, I lost all control. Damn, I could have lost my medical license and thrown my whole career away for that, but it didn't matter, all that I cared about was being with her. Then I had a weekend with her and then she broke my heart."

"We are both intelligent woman, Aimee. How did we allow her to dupe us and take advantage of you and me?"

"Good question. For me I think I was so overwhelmed by her that I couldn't help myself. I will never let that happen to me again." She caressed Elin's cheek. "Not since you came into my life."

"With your help, Aimee, I won't either. Do you think we can?" Elin nodded and blew out a breath.

"I know we can." She held up her wine glass and Elin did the same. When the glasses clinked, Aimee smiled. "Together we are strong and will prevail."

"Yes, we will."

"We must always remember that she is a predator and we are the prey."

"That is a frightening thought." Elin shivered.

"Knowledge is strength, El. We know, therefore we will succeed."

"That we will." Elin reached across the table and ran a finger over Aimee's hand. "I look forward to getting to know you in all ways."

"Really?" Aimee asked with a wink. "*All ways* is good."

Elin grinned. "What do you say we go back to my place?"

"Your place would be fantastic."

†

When they returned from dinner, Elin opened the door to her apartment and smiled at Aimee. "You want to come in or is it too late for you?"

Aimee looked at her watch. "I have to be at the hospital at seven."

"Oh, okay. Some other time maybe."

"Count on it." Aimee put her hands on Elin's hips and pulled her closer.

"I will." Elin let her lips hover over Aimee's before she captured them. Other than Marissa and a few unnamed women in bars, she had never really kissed anyone. She felt Aimee's tongue run across her lips and she opened her mouth to invite it in.

They kissed passionately for what seemed like forever until they heard a door somewhere open and close. Aimee took a step back and grinned.

Elin returned the grin. "I wish you didn't have to go," she whispered.

"Me, too. There's no hurry. We have time to get to know each other first."

"I hope that isn't a long time."

"Oh, trust me, it won't be." Aimee kissed Elin again then moved away. "I'll call you tomorrow."

"I'll look forward to that. Do you want to come for dinner tomorrow? I'll cook."

"Absolutely."

After another quick kiss, Aimee gave her a hug before she left.

That night started Elin on the road to recovery from Marissa Banks by taking her first tentative steps toward finding happiness with Aimee Sullivan.

CHAPTER SIXTEEN

It was Saturday morning and Elin stood at the front window looking at the street below. It was the beginning of summer, and traffic was already heavier than usual. Soon the city would be bustling with sightseers. An Uber stopped outside the building and she smiled when she saw Aimee get out. They had been dating for the last two months and although they hadn't had sex yet, Elin felt as though they were committed to each other. It wasn't that Elin didn't want to be intimate with Aimee—she did—but every time they got close to that moment she'd pull away. Memories of Marissa and her duplicity kept Elin from taking that final step of commitment. The sound of a key in the door had her turning and smiling. She was glad she'd given Aimee a key. It made her feel safe.

"Hey, are you ready for breakfast?"

"Yes, I'm starving."

"How did your night go?"

"Not too good. I stayed with the patient's family, preparing them for what was to come, but when he passed, they were still devastated. The hardest part as always, were the young children, who didn't understand why their father wouldn't wake up." Aimee shook her head. "Over the years I've had to do this and it never gets easier. We learn to be detached and not let our feelings interfere, but I've found that easier said than done."

Elin went to her and pulled Aimee into a hug.

"I've got you," she whispered. Elin kept holding her until Aimee finally gave in to her feelings and cried.

When Aimee pulled away and kissed her, Elin wanted nothing more than to comfort her and kissed Aimee back. The kisses became more insistent and Elin could feel her body wanting more. A hand snaked under her shirt and fingers caressed her breast and it was at that moment Elin pulled away.

"I can't," she sobbed. "I want to, but I just can't. I'm sorry, Aims."

"I know. It's okay, we will get there when the time is right for both of us." Aimee blew out a breath and took a step back.

"But it's not fair to you. I want to be with you in all ways." Elin let out an exasperated breath. "Damn you, Marissa, for doing this to me," she growled. "I hate her."

"So, do I." Aimee lifted Elin's chin. "Did you say something about breakfast? I don't remember eating since lunch yesterday."

Elin took her hand and led them to the kitchen. "How about waffles?"

"My favorite." Aimee leaned in, gave Elin a kiss, and smiled. "Would you like to go to Washington Park today? We can go to the butterfly house."

"I'd love that." Elin hugged Aimee. "First we eat breakfast. I have everything ready and I just need to make the waffles."

†

In all the years that Elin lived in the city, she had never been to Washington Square Park. She had visited Central Park and, in comparison, Washington Square was smaller but held all the charm of a park where she could people-watch. Aimee brought a blanket along with a basket of snacks and drinks. They stood on the edge of the grass like vultures waiting for someone to move so they could claim their grassy spot. Once situated, they sat close and the nearness made Elin tremble.

"Are you cold?" Aimee asked.

"No." Elin bumped Aimee's shoulder with hers. "You make me feel giddy and happy."

"As you do me, Elin." Aimee leaned in and kissed Elin.

Elin pulled back. "We can't do that here. Someone will see us."

"El, look around. Do you see anyone looking at us or doing anything different?"

Elin looked around.

"See, no one is paying us any attention. Relax. I promise not to kiss you again until we get back to your apartment."

"Thank you." Elin went quiet.

"Are you upset with me?"

"What? Why would I be upset?"

"I kissed you in public."

"Don't be silly. I was watching the women to see what they are wearing. I love to do that and imagine how I would dress them." Elin looked at Aimee's disbelieving face. "Okay, I was a little upset that you kissed me, but I can see that you are right, no one is paying attention to us."

"Do you have a particular type you like the best?"

"No." Elin shook her head. "I think all women, no matter what the size or shape, are beautiful. I think that today's fashions cater to women under size eight and then they try to adapt that size to the larger women. It doesn't work." She pointed to a group of women walking by them. "See that last girl?" Aimee nodded. "That's who designers design for."

"Now that you mention it, I know what you mean. Beauty comes in all sizes."

"Exactly. Did you know that in the forties through the sixties the average size of a woman was a twelve? They were voluptuous and all woman."

"Hmm. Rita Hayworth comes to mind along with Marylin Monroe."

"And we can't forget, Jayne Mansfield, Sophia Loren, or Elizabeth Taylor."

"Or the biggest bombshells, Jean Harlow and Mae West." Aimee smiled. "They were something else."

"I wish I could have designed a dress for any of them." Elin gave Aimee a once over. "I'd love to design something for you. You have all the right curves." She could feel her face heat up.

"Do I now?" Aimee grinned and raised her eyebrows. "You have some nice curves yourself."

"Why don't we walk around and see what else is happening in the park," Elin asked, suddenly feeling uncomfortable with the theme of the conversation.

"Great. Let's pack our stuff and see what we can find."

They spent most of the afternoon strolling hand in hand through the park and visiting the butterflies. The butterfly house was everything Elin had thought it would be and more.

"Thank you for suggesting this, Aims. It is so relaxing to just go out and be...I don't know...one of the crowd I guess." Elin stopped and pulled Aimee close and kissed her.

"What do you say we take this back to your apartment?" asked Aimee.

"I say, how fast can you walk?" Elin kissed Aimee again before they headed out of the park.

†

On the way back to Elin's place they passed a pizza shop and Aimee's stomach let out a loud grumble.

"That sure smells good. What do you say we get a pie to take out?"

"Sounds good to me." Elin was happy to agree. When they had left the park, all the signs said they were on the way to making love. That was what she wanted then, but now there were doubts. *It's too soon.* "We can watch a movie with beer and pizza."

"A great way to end a perfect day." Aimee took her hand. "Come on, let's order the pizza."

Elin was relieved that Aimee didn't seem disappointed that they wouldn't be having sex. *Maybe that isn't what she thought and it's only me.*

Back at Elin's apartment, Aimee slid the pizza box on the kitchen table while Elin got out some plates and beers.

"This smells delicious, El. I've never had a margarita pizza before."

"If you like chicken, basil, and cheese, you'll like it." Elin patted Aimee's arm. "Come on, let's eat on the couch while we watch *Ocean's 8*."

"Right behind you." Aimee brought the pizza and, after putting it on the coffee table, sat next to Elin.

"Thank you for the day, Aims. I still can't believe that those two butterflies actually landed on my arm. I could feel the air moving when they flew away. It was awesome."

"It was good to see you so relaxed and happy, El. I know it has been difficult for you the last several months, but hopefully things will take a positive turn for you. How are the designs coming along?"

"Well, Bess is encouraging me to see if we can make a few of my designs and test them out on some of the customers. She said she'd set aside a special area that will feature my clothes."

"Hey, that is great news." Aimee put her arm around Elin's shoulders and pulled her close. "I just know you will take the fashion world by storm."

"From your lips." Elin grinned. "Time to start the movie."

Two hours later the pizza and beer were gone and the movie was over. Aimee yawned and stretched her arms. "I liked that movie and now I need to call an Uber and go home."

"It's late and you had a long day after a longer night. Why not stay here?" Elin wiggled her eyebrows. "Promise I won't bite."

"Best offer I've had in a long time. I am exhausted."

Not too long after, the two women where snuggled in bed.

"Are you okay?" Aimee noticed the worried look on Elin's face. "What are you worrying about?"

"Nothing really."

"You can't fool me that easily, El. If you are worried about having sex, no worries, I am too tired and don't have the energy."

"Well that doesn't say much for my sex appeal," Elin replied with a grin. "Actually I was just thinking."

"By the look on your face, it must be something serious."

"It is, and it isn't."

"Tell me, please."

"She was the only one I ever had sex with. How do I get her out of my mind, Aims, and move on?" Elin asked, snuggling closer. "I want her out of my life."

"Is that what you really want?" Aimee's voice was soft and reassuring.

"After all she did to me, of course I do. I hope she rots in hell and if she doesn't, I hope someone comes along and gives her a taste of her own medicine."

"You didn't answer my question." Aimee bent her arm, lifted her head, and rested it on her hand. She looked at Elin. "Do you really want to be rid of her? Forever?"

"Yes, I do, but I'm the consummate optimist, so I wonder if she will come back and be mine someday."

"I see. You know that will never happen, right?" Aimee rolled on her back and moved away. "Remember I know what you are going through."

"How did you get her out of your mind?" Elin whispered.

"By finding something better to believe in."

"Like what? Your job? Friends? Please tell me."

"Like you, El."

The words were spoken so softly that Elin had to take a moment to process them. "Me?"

"Yes, you. Ever since I first saw you the night that she brought me here, I haven't been able to get you out of my mind. I wanted to claw her eyes out for what she did to you. It was unforgivable that she preyed on you, then cast you aside."

"My protector." Elin leaned over and kissed Aimee. "I think you are my reason, but I need time." She caressed Aimee's cheek. "Is that okay?"

"Not sure about that." Aimee moved away.

"Look, it took you years to get over her. I'm still raw, Aims, can't you see that?" Elin implored while wiping a tear from her eye.

"Don't cry, El. Take your time. I'm not going anywhere but here."

"Promise?"

"Yes." Aimee kissed her soundly.

"Let's get some sleep."

Elin put her arm around Aimee and held her close but couldn't fall asleep. Aimee's words kept scrolling through her mind like a news crawl. Aimee always put Elin first. She was sweet, loveable, kind, supportive, and was always there for her. So why was she hesitant when it came to the physical part of their relationship with Aimee? When they kissed, her body felt tingly and warm. In her heart she knew that Aimee wouldn't hurt her or treat her the way Marissa had. Aimee was everything she could ask for. Elin pulled Aimee closer and kissed her neck before nuzzling closer.

"You asleep?" Elin asked as she continued her assault on Aimee's neck.

"Not anymore. What do you have in mind?" Aimee asked her voice full of emotion.

"Aims, you are my reason."

Aimee turned over and caressed Elin's cheek. "Are you sure?"

"Yes, I want you for always."

"Are you sure?" Aimee asked again when Elin ran a hand over her breasts. "I want this to be very special, not something that will break your heart."

"I trust you, Aims." Elin caressed Aimee's cheek. "Make love with me."

"El, I know your only other experience was with *that* woman. You should know that there are all different kinds of sex, but the two you need to know about are making love and taking a body. The first is tender and kind and thinks of the partner's pleasure, the second is what she did to you and me. There wasn't love or kindness, she just fucked us, that is the only word for it." Aimee watched Elin blow out a sigh of what she thought was acceptance. "I will never treat you that way."

"Promise."

"Yes. When I was growing up my mother was, shall we say, somewhat fanatical about church and the Bible. She'd make us memorize parts of the Bible. This is one that stuck with me all these years later." Aimee paused before continuing.

"Love is patient, love is kind. It does not envy, it does not boast, it is not proud. It does not dishonor others, it is not self-seeking, it is not easily angered, it keeps no record of wrongs. Love does not delight in evil but rejoices with the truth. It always protects, always trusts, always hopes, always perseveres. Love never fails."

Elin moved closer so that their bodies melded into one. She placed a feather light kiss on Aimee's lips before it intensified, and she moaned.

"I want you, Aims. Now."

Aimee slowly removed Elin's clothes and could feel her body shudder as she ran her fingers over the bare skin.

"You are so beautiful," she whispered. For Aimee this was like Elin's first time, ignoring what had happened with Marissa. No one's first time should be taken in a frenzied act that she felt was as close to rape as sex could be. Aimee wanted Elin to know how wonderful and fulfilling sex could be when both partners give and take equally.

Elin closed her eyes as her body reacted to Aimee's gentle touches. It was so unlike the frenetic way Marissa had made love to her. With Aimee, Elin didn't feel like she was going to implode. No, this time her body's need and want intensified with each touch and whispered word, and not in a frenzied fuck. What was happening? It wasn't a rollercoaster ride with ups, downs, twists and turns, like it had been with Marissa, but a slow burning fire that made her tremble and cry out for more. She could feel her body climbing toward an orgasm and whimpered

"Please, I can't hold out much longer."

Her body stiffened and she held her breath as a feeling of pure exhilaration filled her body.

170

"I had no idea," Elin said in a shaky voice.

"That is what it is like when your emotions and not just sex are involved." Aimee pulled her closer and kissed her cheek.

After her body settled and she was wrapped in Aimee's arms, Elin began to cry.

"What's the matter? Did I hurt you?" Aimee had risen on an elbow and looked at her.

"No, you were wonderful." Elin blew out a breath. "I'm just so happy. Do you think we can..." she looked away "...do it again?"

"I think that can be arranged." Aimee pulled her close so that their breasts touched before she kissed Elin soundly.

Elin let out a low growl and began to explore Aimee's body.

It was then that she realized that, unlike Marissa, Aimee focused on making love as a joint experience. She was passionate, loving, and eager to fulfill all of Elin's needs. Elin gradually began to realize the difference between someone loving her and someone using her. Nothing in her experiences with Marissa had prepared her for the deep, loving feelings she had for Aimee. Sex wasn't only about heart-pounding orgasms, but was more about deep feelings of tenderness and love.

CHAPTER SEVENTEEN

Elin walked briskly along the sidewalk toward Boutique La René. If she didn't hurry, she'd be late for her first appointment.

Just as she got to the door her phone rang. When she saw who the caller was, she smiled.

"Good morning, beautiful."

"Hi, sorry I wasn't there when you woke up. As it turned out the emergency wasn't one. How are you?"

"I feel like I'm walking on air. No one has ever made me feel the way you did last night, Aims." Elin could feel her body react to the memory of their night together.

"When I got to the hospital and found out I didn't need to be there, I wanted to jump in a cab and come back to you."

"Why didn't you?"

"I didn't want to seem too anxious," Aimee whispered. "You said you wanted to go slow and—"

"Aimee, that was weeks ago. After last night I don't want slow anymore. I want you."

"Damn." Just then the door to the boutique opened and Bess stared at her.

"Are you coming in? Ms. Jacobson should be here shortly."

"Hold on a minute, Aims." Elin looked at her boss. "I have everything ready for her, Bess. This call is important and once I've finished, I will be in. No worries."

"Okay, but hurry if you can." Bess gave Elin a curious look.

After Elin nodded to Bess she said, "Okay, I'm back."

"Did I hear right? Did you just blow off Bess?" Aimee laughed.

"Yes I did. You are far more important. Will I see you for dinner?"

"Is that what you want?"

"Hmm, let's see…I want you," Elin whispered.

"As I do you. I'll be there."

"Bring a change of clothes. I don't plan on letting you leave until tomorrow morning."

"I like the sound of that. See you later."

"Bye." Elin turned and pushed open the door. She quickly walked to her work room with Bess following close behind.

"Okay, out with it. What's going on?" Bess asked.

"Nothing that I know of." Elin struggled to keep a bubble of happiness from escaping. She was floating on air and didn't want to come down or share what she was feeling.

Bess's eyes were boring into her, and when that happened it was hard to not speak.

"Well, something or someone is responsible for the glow on your face. Give."

Elin looked at the floor. Bess was her friend and mentor but for now Elin wanted to keep Aimee to herself. She knew if she looked up Bess would have her arms crossed and still be looking at her. A knock on the door made her look up.

"Elin, Ms. Jacobson is here," Camille said.

"Thank you, Camille. I'll be right there." Elin looked at Bess. "Sorry, I need to go."

"My office for lunch."

"I'll be there." Elin left the room knowing that there was no way she'd be getting out of telling Bess about Aimee.

†

Elin hesitantly tapped on Bess's office. When she heard "enter," she opened the door.

"Ah, Elin, please sit down. I have cob salads for us. What would you like to drink?"

"Water will be fine." Elin took a seat at the small table that was off to the left of the room and where they usually ate lunch.

Bess smiled and after placing the water on the table, she sat opposite Elin. "Okay, spill. What's going on with you?"

"Well..." Elin paused. She had been thinking all morning about how to share her relationship with Aimee. From the start, Bess had been there for her, supporting all she did. Bess deserved the truth or as much as Elin was willing to share. "I've met someone."

"I knew it," Bess said triumphantly. "The bloom of new love was the giveaway."

"Wait, I didn't say 'love.' We are in the early days."

"Please tell me more."

"What do you want to know?" Elin really didn't want to say more but knew a few facts wouldn't hurt.

"How did you meet?"

"We met through a mutual acquaintance. She's a doctor and really cute."

"Anything else? Surely there is more to tell. Did you tell your folks? How does your mother feel about you dating a woman?"

"They know. When I first told my mom, she wasn't happy but she realized it's who I am and she accepted it. It took some time but in the end it worked out."

"But, she's still not happy? Or at least that is how it sounds."

"She is and she isn't." Elin looked away. "Would you be?"

"Ideally we want our children to be happy, and we worry about them from the day they are born. We want to protect them from the pitfalls life has in store for them. Any time you pick a lifestyle that is not the norm there will be problems." Bess shrugged. "I think that is what your mother objects to…people ridiculing you."

"She does understand that times have changed, and it is now…what do they call it? Gender fluid." Elin shook her head and laughed. "Aimee, that's her name, and I were in the park yesterday and we held hands. No one batted an eye. At first I was worried someone would say something but when I realized we weren't the only ones, I relaxed."

"So, this is pretty serious?"

"Like I said, Bess, it is the early days, and I don't want to say too much and spoil it."

"Fair enough, but I hope to be a bridesmaid at the wedding." Bess grinned then dug into her salad. "Maybe even matron of honor."

"You're incorrigible. Trust me, Bess, you will be the first person I ask if, and it's a big if, I get married." Elin laughed, then began to eat her salad too.

"How's your collection coming along?" Bess asked.

"I am working on refining what I've done so far."

"Any problems I can help you with?" Bess looked at her directly.

"Not really. The biggest thing is thinking forward and that means I need to do lots of studying on the latest trends. Then I will work at anticipating how they will change."

"Have you enlisted Sarah's help?"

"Yes, and she is willing to work on the patterns I come up with as prototypes." Elin gave Bess a crooked smile. "We shall see."

"I've seen the designs and your work is first class. Keep at it and I know you will be successful." Bess reached out and put her hand over Elin's.

"I've worked all my life toward that goal, and I won't stop now. It will just take time." Elin lifted her eyebrows and grinned. "The big question is…how much time will it take."

"Come show me what you have done so far and we will see if we can work out a timeline for completion." Bess stood and smiled.

"I don't think it is as easy as that."

"No, it isn't, but it is a start and once you have that, the rest is a piece of cake. Come on, we have eight months before the next Fashion Week."

"Seriously, Bess. Fashion Week? There's no way—"

"Leave it up to me, Elin." Bess grinned. "I haven't been in the fashion business all this time to not have contacts that can make things happen. Trust me, I've seen your designs and I know what sells. You, my dear, have what it takes and you deserve to be at Fashion Week."

"From your lips, Bess." Elin shook her head and laughed.

†

It was Elin's day to reveal to Bess her completed designs and samples. For the last four months Elin and Sarah Hamilton, the store's seamstress, had worked on converting the designs into a finished collection.

"Elin!" Bess exclaimed as Elin walked in the door. "I couldn't help myself. I had to take a peek at your collection." Bess put her hand over her heart. "They are all exquisite."

"Didn't we have an appointment for me to show you the line?" Elin scrunched her face in confusion.

"I know, dear, but I just couldn't wait. I don't think I slept at all last night." Bess moved closer and wrapped Elin in a hug. "I am so excited for you."

"Thank you. I just wish you would have waited for me to show you so I could see your reaction." Elin could feel her insides shiver. "Did you really like them?" She held her breath.

"Oh, yes, dear. From the cursory look I took, wow is the word that came to my mind."

"Really?" Elin could see the sincerity on Bess's face and she was over the moon with happiness. "Oh, Bess, you like them, that is so wonderful. I can't believe it, all my dreams are coming true."

"Yes they are." Bess smiled and gave Elin a light hug. "Now that you are here, my dear, will you please give me the complete rundown, and maybe even model some for me."

"Sure." Elin shook her head. She was a little upset that Bess had looked at her designs without her, but at the same time relieved that Bess liked them. She was endearing and Elin knew Bess supported her one hundred percent.

"Give me a few minutes to get settled and make a phone call. Then we can go over everything."

"You know, I think I will call in a favor or two and have a couple of models come in so you can see everything as a spectator. I think that will give you a better idea of what you might need to change. Though, from what I saw, I don't think you will need to do much."

"That is a great idea, Bess. Thank you."

"Certainly, dear. I will let you know the timing once I've set things up."

Elin nodded and went to her office shaking her head. Was this really happening? She had worked all her life toward this goal, but was it her time? She was still young and she had so much more to learn. Thoughts of the designs and what-ifs kept bombarding her mind, making her dizzy.

"Aimee, I need to call her."

Elin pulled her phone out of her pocket and pressed a few buttons before she heard the sound of ringing.

"Hi, are you okay?" Aimee asked in a worried voice.

"Yes, yes, I am. I know you're busy with patients, but I wanted you to know. Bess loves my designs and is going to bring in a model so we can see how they'd look in a show."

"El, that is wonderful. When is this happening?"

"Later today I think. Bess is going to tell me when she gets it all arranged."

"I'm so happy for you. Sounds like we need to celebrate tonight. How about instead of you cooking, I take my favorite girl to dinner?"

"I'd like that." Elin heard something that sounded like an alarm go off in the background.

"Hey, we've got one coming in so I need to go. I'll see you later."

"Okay, bye." Elin ended the call and held her phone close. How had she gotten so lucky as to have Aimee in her life at this monumental moment? She quickly punched in another number.

"Mom, guess what…"

CHAPTER EIGHTEEN

Elin left work early so she could stop at the market on the way home to pick up something for dinner. She and Aimee had been dating for five months and recently had been spending most nights at either her apartment or Aimee's. Tonight she planned on surprising her lover with something special and wanted the meal to be perfect. Elin pushed a squeaking cart up and down the aisles until she spotted shrimp and decided to make one of Aimee's favorite meals—shrimp and sausage with peppers and zucchini. A bottle of white wine along with some mixed greens rounded out the items for dinner. Now for dessert. The thought made her smile for she knew exactly what she wanted for dessert—Aimee.

Once she was back home, Elin set to chopping the veggies and sausage before shelling the shrimp and dusting it with bay seasoning. She still had to set up the surprise she had for Aimee, and she needed everything to be prepped for cooking so she'd have enough time. With only the actual cooking left, Elin hurried into the bedroom to change her clothes, all the while rehearsing how she'd surprise Aimee. Should she just take her hand and show her, or say nothing and let her find out herself? She heard the door open and she smiled. Aimee was home.

"Guess I'll play it by ear," Elin said to herself.

"I'm home." Aimee called out as she entered the apartment.

"I'm here." Elin came out of the bedroom and smiled at her lover.

"You're the only one I wanted to see." Aimee pulled Elin into her arms. "How was your day?"

"Took off early so I could make your favorite meal. Do you realize that today is the anniversary of when we first met?"

"Really? Five months right?" Aimee hugged Elin tighter.

Elin leaned back slightly and gently kissed Aimee. It didn't take long for the kisses to intensify.

"Hey, we'd better stop now so I can finish making dinner. Then, my dear, I plan on having you for dessert."

"I like the sound of that."

"Well, let me finish up in the kitchen. Why don't you open a bottle of wine for us?"

"That was delicious." Aimee pushed back from the table and began collecting the plates.

181

"No, don't do that." Elin got up quickly and went around to Aimee. "I need to show you something."

"Can it wait? It won't take long for me to put the dishes in the dishwasher." Aimee saw the disappointed look on Elin's face. "Hey, that can wait, what do you have?"

"Thank you." Elin grinned and took Aimee's hand. "Come with me."

"What's going on?" Aimee asked when she entered the bedroom.

Elin walked over to the dresser of drawers and pulled two of them open. "Drawers for you." She then went to the closet and waved across a partial empty clothes rod. "And closet space."

"You want me to move in?" Aimee couldn't believe what she was seeing.

"Yes...no...I want you to have your own space here so you know this is where you belong."

Aimee could see Elin's facial expression droop and her shoulders sag.

"I've overstepped, haven't I?" Elin swiped at her eyes.

"No, no you didn't. I'm just surprised that's all. It's something I never expected." Aimee was at Elin's side immediately and hugged her close. "Thank you, El, it is a wonderful surprise. I've always wanted a drawer."

"Are you sure? You don't seem to be," Elin shrugged, "very enthusiastic."

"I am. You're not going to believe this, El, but I had the same idea and emptied a drawer for you...you surprised me first that's all. Great minds and all that."

"You really did?"

"Yes. I had a patient yesterday who died and her daughter said, 'I never got to tell her I had cleaned out a room for her to come live with me.' It got me to thinking that I want you to feel like you belong in my place." Aimee shrugged and walked slowly toward Elin and put her arms around her lover. "I want you in my life, El, for always."

"Wow." Elin looked up at Aimee. "For always?"

"Yes."

"I don't know what to say. To be honest it terrifies me."

"What does?"

"Always." Elin took a step back and Aimee let go. "Will you give me some time?"

"Of course." Aimee saw the confused and scared look on Elin's face. "Do you want me to leave?"

"Yes. Do you mind? I have some thinking to do. You are too much of a distraction and I need alone time right now."

"Sure, no problem." Aimee hugged Elin close and kissed her on the cheek. I'll see you tomorrow. Okay?"

"Of course." Elin looked at her with a weak smile. "See you tomorrow."

Aimee stood at the landing outside Elin's apartment, looking at the door she had closed behind her. She tried to wrap her mind around what had just happened. Elin's gesture was sweet and full of a multitude of unspoken words of commitment. Why had she reacted that way? With a tentative step she started back toward the closed door then stopped. The vision of Elin's haunted look confused her. She'd give Elin the time she asked for and would call her tomorrow. She needed to fix things. First she needed to know what the things were.

"Damn you, Marissa, you did this to her."

Elin heard the door close and the quiet snick of the lock engaging and sobbed. Aimee wanted *always* and that terrified her. Why couldn't she completely trust Aimee? In all their months together Aimee had shown her nothing but tenderness and kindness, yet Elin was having a hard time believing that she really meant *always*. That was a huge commitment. She had no idea what made her afraid but she was. Then, the answer was suddenly clear. Her experience with Marissa was still coloring everything and she was allowing that to happen.

"Idiot," she cried while punching her pillow. She stared at the ceiling and slowed her breathing until she fell into a light restless sleep. Elin didn't know what woke her up until she heard the familiar beeping that meant she had a text message. She felt around to find her jeans, pulled her phone out of a back pocket, and looked to see who had sent the message. Aimee. Elin shook her head and clicked on the button.

El, I'm sorry. I don't know what made you so scared. What I do know is that I want you in my life and will gladly take the offered drawers and closet space. Please talk to me. I'm outside your door.

At that moment Elin knew she needed to make a decision. Let Aimee in or let fear and Marissa rule her life. She went to the door, flung it open, and watched Aimee walk slowly into the room, closing the door behind her.

"Can I start again? Obviously my saying the word 'always' spooked you. That never was my intention."

"I know that. I overreacted."

"El, like you, I haven't had a lot of encounters with women. I was always too busy with my career for that. I think that Marissa soured both of us on relationships in general, making us fearful of letting anyone into our lives."

"Yep, I agree with that." Elin could feel her shoulders relax at Aimee's words.

"El, I'm not Marissa and never will be. I think we have something special between us and I'd like to continue exploring that possibility."

Elin looked at Aimee with amazement. She was speaking to her heart and Elin could feel it warm to the words. She was speechless.

"I've been standing out there by your door, afraid that I made a mess of things by letting you know how I feel about you." Aimee took a few steps closer then stopped. "The last thing I want is to never hold you in my arms again."

"If you'll accept my drawer I'll accept yours." Elin gathered Aimee in her arms and held her tight before kissing her softly. "You know this means were going steady."

"Well, we are going to look rather silly walking around with a drawer on our finger." Aimee laughed.

"Then there will be no mistaking who you belong to."

"You're the only one."

Elin pressed her lips to Aimee's before she ran her tongue over her lips.

Aimee ended the kiss. "What do you say we take this into the bedroom?"

"I'd like that," Elin whispered. "We should never go to sleep angry, and trust me I'm not angry, only wanting you."

"I like the sound of that."

Elin took Aimee's hand and walked with her into the bedroom.

†

"The upside to fights is making up," a sated Elin said, holding Aimee close. She rolled over on top of her lover.

"Yes it is." Aimee kissed Elin's nose. "About the drawer thing—"

"Let's not go there again." She kissed Aimee's nose. "I can think of better things to do."

"All I wanted to say is that, if we shared an apartment, we wouldn't have to have drawers."

"Really? You want us to live together?" Elin rolled onto the mattress, then sat up letting the sheet fall off.

"Yes. Don't you think it is about time?"

"Yes I do." Elin put her hands on her cheeks. "I can't believe this. You know we'll have to get a different apartment. I don't think either of ours is big enough for two."

"Funny thing you should say that." Aimee grinned. "My aunt lives in a rent-controlled apartment about ten blocks from here and she is moving to assisted living. She said I can have the apartment. It has three bedrooms, a living room, dining room, two full baths, and a kitchen."

"That sounds fantastic but can we afford something like that?"

"No worries." Aimee tapped Elin's nose. "Remember I said rent control. We will not only be able to afford it, but we'll have money left over."

"Perfect." Elin hugged Aimee. "Will you meet my parents?" she asked tentatively.

"Of course. How about this weekend? I have it off."

†

Aimee drove her Jeep up the long curved driveway and parked in front of the three-car garage. The house was a

Garrison Colonial surrounded by what she estimated was an acre of ground. Elin's parents obviously didn't lack money. That was curious since Elin never acted as if she were privileged. On the contrary, she was no doubt one of the most down-to-earth women she'd ever met. She looked at Elin who seemed to be apprehensive.

"Do they know you are bringing me as your partner and not a man?"

"Yes. I told them not long ago that I was now dating a woman."

"How did they take that?"

"As you'd expect. But," Elin let out a slight chuckle, "when I said I was dating a doctor they seemed happy."

"Ah, you played the doctor card. Well done." Both women laughed.

"Come on, let's get this over with." Elin opened her door and Aimee followed suit.

"You sure I look okay?"

"Yes. You look fine. I doubt that either of my parents are in anything but jeans."

Just as they reached the door a car came up the driveway.

"Shit," Elin said. "They asked my brother and sister too."

"So, it is a family affair you've brought me to." Aimee wrinkled her forehead. "Wait till I take you to meet my family. There are nine of us."

The door opened and Elin's mother opened her arms wide and pulled her daughter to her. "I'm so glad you're here, Sunny." She then turned to Aimee. "You must be Aimee. I've heard so much about you. I'm glad you're here too."

"Mrs. Prescott, it's good to meet you. Thank you for inviting me." Aimee held out her hand.

"Please call me Dorothy." She took Aimee's hand. "I'm glad you could make it, Aimee. Elin tells me you're an ER doctor."

"Yes, ma'am, I am."

"Come on in and meet my husband—oh, I see Robby and Patty are here. George, the kids are here."

George Prescot came and pulled Elin into a hug. "I'm glad you could come." He looked at Aimee. "And who do we have here?"

Just then Elin's brother and sister walked up to them.

"Hi, sis," Elin's brother Robby said.

"Hi. I see we are *all* here," Elin said sarcastically. "Aimee, this my brother Robby, and my sister Patty."

Elin took her hand and Aimee swallowed the nerves that suddenly had her stomach roiling. Nevertheless, she put on her best doctor's face and politely shook each hand. To Aimee's surprise none of them seemed to be fazed by the fact that she was introduced as "my girlfriend." That was until Elin's grandparents arrived.

"Okay, I see they are here too. This should be good." Elin shook her head. "I promise that I thought it was only my parents and us. I'm sorry. My grandparents came here in their twenties from Sweden, but are still old fashioned in their thinking, so be ready for their frowns when I tell them you are my girlfriend."

"Not a problem," Aimee said, not meaning it at all.

"Grandpop, Granny, this is my girlfriend, Dr. Aimee Sullivan."

"A doctor of what?" Elin's grandpop asked harshly.

"I am an emergency room doctor, sir."

"You know when I had my heart problems I went to the emergency room and a lovely young woman doctor took

188

good care of me." Grandpop, took Aimee's hand and kissed her cheek. "I am most happy to meet you."

"As I am you." Aimee smiled and then Elin's Granny, Anna, hugged her. Once the couple left to get a drink Aimee let out a deep sigh.

"No worries, Aims, if Pops likes you then you're in."

"Thank God. When they walked in and I saw them, I thought things were going too smoothly for me." Aimee laughed. "I thought he was going to tell me I should be at home taking care of my husband and kids."

The eight of them sat around an old, round, oak table in the kitchen, enjoying a meal of pot roast and potatoes. The chatter around Aimee made her relax until she heard a booming voice that stopped all talk.

"George, get the glögg. It is time to celebrate." Elin's grandpop, who had to be in his eighties, bellowed in a strong take-charge voice.

"Should I be afraid?" Aimee whispered to Elin.

"No."

"In our family, Doctor Aimee, we welcome new members by all sharing in a drink that has been passed down from my father and his father," Pops said.

Aimee gave the man a smile and watched as Elin's dad came in with a tray full of small cups and a steaming pot. He poured the glögg into each cup and passed them out.

"Today we celebrate Doctor Aimee who is joining our family." Robert raised his cup and said, "Skål," before he took a drink.

Everyone around the table clinked their cups and cheered "skål" before taking a drink.

"You are now an official member of the family," Elin said. "How does it feel?"

189

"I'm overwhelmed." It wasn't long before everyone was coming up to her and giving her a kiss of welcome.

†

Back in their new apartment, Aimee sat on the couch and snuggled close to Elin.

"Today was nice. I like your family, they all were friendly."

"My grandpop told me you were a keeper. Granny didn't say much but I think she will come around at some point. One thing I know about Swedes is that they are stubborn." Elin laughed.

"Good to know. Does that particular trait mean I can expect you to dig your heels in from time to time?"

"Probably."

"Be right back." Aimee got up and walked quickly away. Just as fast, she came back and stood in front of Elin. "I had a long talk with your dad while you were helping your mom in the kitchen." She bent down on one knee and held out a ring box.

"Elin Prescot, I love you. Will you do me the honor of marrying me?"

"Yes, Aimee, yes." Elin pulled Aimee to her and gave her a searing kiss. When they came up for air, Elin smiled. "I take it my dad said it was okay?"

"Both your dad and mom said, 'welcome to the family' and gave me their blessing."

"Oh, Aims, you make me so happy." Elin got up, left the room, returned quickly and got down on one knee, and opened a velvet box. "Aimee Sullivan, I love you. Will you do me the honor of being my wife?"

190

"Yes, I will." It was Aimee's turn to initiate the kisses before she stopped and smiled. "You know we've always been on the same wavelength in almost everything." She took the ring and slid it on Elin's finger.

Elin then took her ring and placed it on Aimee's finger. "Now 'always' is official."

"I'd like a spring wedding," Aimee said.

"It's a time of renewal and beginning again. I like the thought of that." Elin smiled. "Do we want a big wedding?"

"If it is up to me I'd say let's go to Vegas or the court house."

"Me too. The only problem with that is all my family will want to be there."

"Then we will have small wedding with family and close friends. Of course there are nine in my family but I doubt any of them will come."

"Why? You've never said much about them."

"They don't approve of my lifestyle and pretty much told me if I didn't change not to bother them." Aimee shrugged. "I doubt if I call them and tell them our news they'll be happy for us."

"Oh, Aimee, I'm so sorry." Elin pulled her into a hug. "No worries, as my grandpop said, you are now part of the family."

"I like that."

"Good. Now I need to call my folks and tell them the good news as I am sure they have been waiting by the phone."

"Not yet," Aimee said. "I have other plans for us right now."

"You do, do you? And may I ask what that is?"

"I'd rather show you." Aimee stood and took Elin's hand and led her into the bedroom.

CHAPTER NINETEEN

The time had finally arrived. Elin and Sarah had worked long hours perfecting all the designs for today's women. They also had added several evening gowns to the collection. In two short weeks Elin would know the fate of her lifelong dream. For six years, Bess allowed Elin to work to have her brand name, *Elin,* resonate in the fashion world. Standing behind the curtain as model after model strolled down the runway wearing her creations, she recalled the moment her brand became a reality…

Elin walked toward the store. She had been gone for ten days on her honeymoon after the wedding. The wedding had been everything she dreamed of. She smiled remembering Pops who had insisted that he be the one to walk Aimee down the aisle. All her family were in attendance. Aimee had called her mother and invited her family to the wedding, but none attended. Despite that, everyone had a wonderful time and the memories of the happy event still lingered as she walked into Boutique La René

"Elin, you're back." Bess gave her a tight squeeze. "I had such a good time at your wedding. The girls here are still talking about it."

"It's good to be back. I do have to admit I miss Cabo and the beaches. We were on the water so every night we went to sleep with the sound of the waves. It was very relaxing."

"Which you so nicely reminded us all by the pictures you sent in emails." Bess grinned. "Someday maybe Bill and I will go. Yeah right, all the kids and grandkids will want to go too."

"You wouldn't want it any other way, Bess."

"No, I wouldn't." Bess gave her a Cheshire cat smile. "I have something to show you."

"What? I finally have a new chair in my office?"

"Better." Bess laughed. "Follow me."

Elin followed Bess down the wall where all the samples from different designers were displayed. Above each collection was the designer's name and Elin stopped and held her hand over her mouth when she saw a collection with the Elin name above it.

"Oh, Bess," she said in awe."

"I take it that you like it."

"No, Bess, I love it. You did this for me?"

"Yes. I believe in you and your brand. In fact, we sold two of your suits while you were gone."

"I can't believe it." Elin shook her head trying to take it all in.

"Now all you have to do is keep designing and adding to the collection. Mark my words, you will make it big in the fashion world."

"From your lips to God's ears," Elin whispered. "I actually did some drawings while we were gone." She grinned. "They have all been Aimee approved."

"And how is the good doctor?"

"She is wonderful. I don't know how I got so lucky to have her in my life, much less be married to her."

"She told me almost the same thing at the wedding," Bess said. "I am happy for you but unfortunately we have to get back to work. Your first client, Mrs. Truman, is due at ten thirty."

"Thank you, Bess, for everything. Without your support I don't know that," she pointed to her name above them, "would ever have happened this soon."

Bess hugged her again before they both went off in different directions.

†

Establishing the Elin brand among the Boutique La René clients had been a no-brainer, but new horizons were needed to move to the heady heights of reaching more than the clientele here. The question became, after three years as a brand, did she need to consider going out on her own to achieve it? Elin decided to surprise her wife and take her for a four-day weekend break to a ski resort that she'd been given a free pass to from one of her clients. It would give her time to think about her options. Aims could always be relied upon to give her sound advice. She was Elin's rock in any storm and she loved her more and more each day.

†

When Elin returned to work on the following Tuesday, Bess gave her some wonderful news...

On one cold and bright January day, one of Bess's clients that had been with her for years, Marie Baltz, came into the boutique.

"Marie, welcome," Bess greeted her after Camille showed her to the office. "How have you and your family been?"

"Fantastic in all ways," Marie gushed. "Did you see Kelly's nomination?"

"Yes, I did." Bess pictured Marie's movie-star daughter who was just nominated for an Oscar. "Please tell her congratulations for me."

"I will. How is your family, Bess?"

"They are all good. It's hard to keep up with all their comings and goings. May I take your coat?" Bess stood behind the woman and helped her off with her coat before hanging it up. "Are you ready for your spring selection?"

"Yes, but I'd also like to make an appointment with your Elin for tomorrow."

"Elin? Unfortunately, she's away until Tuesday. Let me check her appointment schedule for next week" Bess consulted the computer. "Hmm, the only thing open is first thing Wednesday, at nine o'clock. Will that work?"

"Give me a moment to text my daughter and see if she is available then."

Bess watched her client tap on her phone as it dawned on her why they wanted an appointment. When Marie turned to her, Bess held her breath.

"Yes, Kelly can be here at that time."

"Excellent. May I ask what she is looking for so Elin can prepare for her?"

Marie grinned. "She needs a gown for the Oscars and I told her all about your upcoming designer Elin and she wanted me to make an appointment. Kelly said that anyone can show up in a de la Renta, Versace, or Wang and she wanted something different and unique."

"If that is what she wants, then Elin is the right designer for her."

†

Elin sat at her desk trying to calm her nerves. In the years that Elin had worked at Boutique La René her clients and those of the others were CEOs, senators, entrepreneurs, governors, and other positions in the country. One of Elin's clients had a minor role in a television series but no one had been a genuine Hollywood A-list movie star. Until now. A knock on the door had her heartbeat increasing.

"Come in." Elin stood and went to the door.

"She's here," Camille said. "Are you ready for me to bring her back?"

"Sure, show her in."

"She's even more beautiful than she is in the movies," Camille said as she left.

The next knock had Elin's heart racing. She took a deep breath and opened the door. "Ms. Baltz, it is good to meet you." Elin held out her hand and was surprised by the warmth and strength of Kelly Marie Baltz's handshake.

"It is my pleasure to meet you Elin…may I call you Elin?"

"Of course." Elin was confused. Wasn't she the one who asked that question? "Please come in and tell me how I can help you."

"I have an idea of what I want, but it is hard to explain," Kelly said.

"Why don't you tell me what you were thinking and we will work together to make it happen."

An hour later they had the makings of the gown Kelly had envisioned.

"I think I have an idea now, Kelly. Do you think you could return tomorrow afternoon? I should have a refined drawing and we can tweak it some if you like it."

"Well, let me see." Kelly pulled out her phone and looked at it. "I can't come back until around five thirty at the earliest. Six would probably be better."

"I can be here then but I won't be able to stay more than forty-five minutes. I have plans go with my wife to a hospital function at seven thirty."

Kelly had a perplexed look. "How long will it take to make the gown?"

"If we come to an agreement on what you want in the way of the gown, and the type of material you'd like, then we can get done in around four weeks, which will give you plenty of time before the Oscars. Once we know all the particulars, then we will do measurements and purchase the material. Since this is a custom piece we will require several fitting dates so it will be perfect for you." Elin smiled. "I know it is overwhelming at first but we will make the process as easy as possible for you. I'll even come to your home if that is necessary." Elin held her breath.

"That sounds reasonable to me. The Oscars are at the end of February. Will you have enough time?"

"You will be my priority."

"And the cost?"

"If you will mention Elin designs when you are on the red carpet and any other time that you are asked about your gown, there will be no cost."

Kelly stood and held out her hand. "Then it is a deal. I will sign any papers necessary tomorrow afternoon. I will try to be here as soon as I can."

"Sounds like a plan to me," Elin said, shaking the offered hand. "I look forward to working with you, Kelly. I will show you out."

Kelly went on to win the Academy Award and made sure that everyone knew about Elin's designs. It didn't take long before new clients were coming into Boutique La René that had the exclusive rights to the Elin line of clothes.

CHAPTER TWENTY

"Elin, Elin over here." The designer turned before she went backstage and smiled as a flash went off.

"Elin," the reporter said following her. "One more question, what do you attribute your successful show to?"

She stopped and considered the question. "There were many events that lead to this night but the two defining moments were when Bess Matthews hired me at Boutique La René and when Kelly Marie Baltz wore my creation to the Oscars."

Elin basked in the glow of the success as her first major show featuring the ELIN line of clothing concluded. The reception following the showing included dignitaries, friends, models, fashion reporters, and other well-wishers. She turned when she felt a tap on her shoulder.

"Bess, can you believe it?" Elin embraced her friend who was instrumental in arranging and running the show. "This never would have happened without you."

"Elin, I am so proud of you." Bess stepped back and gave her protégée a once over. "You are glowing. Success agrees with you."

"It agrees with you too, Bess, I don't—"

Bess interrupted by patting Elin's hand. "You were always destined for this." She extended her hand to the woman by Elin's side. "It's good to see you again, Doctor."

"You too, Bess, you do know I have a name beyond doctor, right?" Aimee took the proffered hand, grinned, and raised her glass. "If you two will excuse me, I will get us all refills." Aimee kissed Elin's cheek. "Be right back."

Bess turned back to Elin. "Things have been so crazy these past months with you off-site putting the final touches on your designs that I keep forgetting to tell you who came in to the shop asking for you when you were away on your ski weekend. "

"Who?"

"Your very first client...what was her name?"

"Marissa Banks." Elin answered immediately and virtually choked on her breath, straightened, gulped deeply, and searched the crowd for Aimee. "Really?" Her eyes kept looking for her wife.

"She harassed Camille, demanding to see you. When I came out to see what the problem was, she told me she would only do business with you. She acted like you were her personal property, demanding to know where you were." Bess' derisive laugh made Elin look directly at her.

"What do you mean?" She saw Aimee making her way toward them and Elin let out a breath.

"There was no way I was going to tell her anything about you. I never did like her, and thought even less of her when she tried to intimidate Camille and myself into revealing where you were. Now mind you, I wanted to tell her about your upcoming show, but I wouldn't give her that satisfaction."

Elin's body calmed as Aimee appeared and placed an arm around her.

"You two look way too serious for such a wonderful day. What's going on?"

Elin eased back into Aimee's reassuring arm. "Nothing, we were just talking about old times." She looked wistfully around the room. "It's kinda hard to believe this is real."

"Oh, it is," Bess said, patting Elin's arm. "And, you deserve every minute of it, dear, so relax and enjoy the ride."

"I will, Bess, thank you for not only all the time and hard work you put into making this a success, but for the faith and trust you put in me over the years. This never would have happened without you."

When Elin saw the publicist Bess had hired waving at her, she sighed. "No rest for the weary. I need to mingle. Please excuse me."

Bess watched Elin walk away before turning to Aimee. "For a time in the early days, I was really worried about her." She touched Aimee's arm. "Thank you for coming into her life. She's blossomed so much since meeting you, and I know it's you and only you." Bess smiled.

Aimee nodded. "It works both ways. She's made a big difference in my life. I don't know how I existed before she came along."

"You are a perfect couple." Bess saw Aimee's eyes focus on Elin.

"What were you two talking about? I can tell something is bothering her."

"We were just talking about our clients." Bess swallowed hard. She didn't know if Aimee knew about Marissa Banks and she certainly wasn't going to spill the beans.

"Will you excuse me, Bess?"

"Certainly." Bess watched Aimee thread through the crowd toward Elin.

†

Elin finally allowed herself to relax as satisfaction crept over her face while she shook the hand of the last guest to leave. Brenda Baxter, her assistant, scurried around the room picking up glasses and plates.

"Brenda, leave those. The caterers will take care of them tomorrow."

"Are you sure? I don't mind."

"Yep, why don't you go home, and I will see you on Monday."

"Okay, if you're sure."

"I am, now get going."

"Have I told you lately how much I love you and how proud I am of you?" Aimee wrapped her arms around her waist.

"Hmm, I think I heard you say that about," Elin answered, lifting her arm and looking at her wristwatch, "five hours ago."

Aimee nestled closer and kissed Elin's neck. "So, what were you and Bess talking about that got you so upset?"

Elin pulled Aimee's hands apart then turned to face her wife. "She said Marissa had been in six months ago looking for me."

"Well that would be a mood buster. What else did she say?" Aimee laughed sarcastically.

"Not much really." Elin's eyes saddened. "Will she ever go away? It's been years since either of us heard from her and here, on my big day, she's back."

"Remember we have our support group." Aimee pulled Elin closer, so she rested on her shoulder.

"I do remember, darling. You gave me hope and love when I thought I didn't deserve it." Elin kissed Aimee. "Thank you for saving me."

"I think it was mutual. Come on, let's go home and celebrate privately."

Elin took Aimee's hand and together they left for their home.

†

Elin opened her eyes and stretched. The night before was a wonderful success. All her dreams for becoming a fashion designer had come true. Her eyes tracked to the empty pillow beside her.

"Aimee?"

"Good morning, beautiful." Aimee came into the bedroom carrying a tray laden with breakfast. "Bet you're hungry this morning. I have all your favorites."

Sitting up with a pillow propped behind her back, Elin's eyes grew wide as Aimee placed a tray over her lap. "Who else is joining us?"

"Not to worry, my dear, I know you can eat it all." She gave Elin a quick kiss before she moved around to the other side of the bed. "Mind if I join you?" Snuggling up close to Elin, she snagged a piece of toast before picking up the paper. "Shall we see what's exciting in the fashion section of the newspaper?" She flipped through the various sections before dramatically opening the style section.

"Come on, let me see too," Elin begged.

"All in good time, darlin'." Aimee positioned the paper away from Elin's view and smiled slyly.

"So, what does it say?"

"Well, there is an interesting article on how to dress appropriately for a wedding." She continued to peruse the page. "Oh, and there's one here about some new designer."

"Aimee!"

Aimee leaned over and kissed Elin's cheek. "Since you asked so nicely, I will read it to you."

Has Elin Prescot arrived? Has she crossed the threshold from promising newcomer into a style establishment? Those uncertain of her fate when they turned up Saturday afternoon at her first big runway show had only to glance at the parade of models in stylish fashions to make up their minds. The new darling of the fashion world is sure to be a favorite of not only the business world but of the ladies' lunch set too. Her designs are fresh, affordable classics, with a bit more of an edge than Ralph Lauren. For the winter season, she focused on party dresses of the breezy romantic variety, but for the spring has branched out into daywear. She has married light-weight leg-elongating trousers with tiny knit sweaters, and added adorable drop-waist dresses in breezy cotton-silk that look just right with flat sandals. When Prescot came out the end of the show for her bow, a standing ovation greeted her as the models made one last lap down the runway. The accolades that will come to this talented young lady are all well-deserved. The mass appeal of the line should have Prescot's ever-growing following coming back for more. To see more, visit Boutique La René.

"There you have it, babe, you've arrived." Aimee put the tray on the floor then pulled Elin in close. "I am so proud of you."

"I couldn't have done it without you."

"Sure you could, you were always destined for great things."

"I may have been, but that all would have been buried if you hadn't come into my life. I was devastated and I didn't want to go on until I saw you standing at my door, and after that everything in my world changed "

"As you changed mine." Aimee kissed the top of Elin's head and sighed happily. "Remember that day when you first showed me your designs?"

"Yes." Elin laughed...

They had been talking to each other daily since their first dinner date. Several times a week they would meet and go out to the theater, dinner, or visit the city's numerous museums. After they had known each other for two months, they shared a picnic lunch in a park across the street from Elin's apartment.

Aimee asked, "What are you dreams?"

"I've always wanted to have my own line of clothing."

"So why haven't you done that? You certainly have the education and training for that."

"I'm afraid. What if I fail?" Shrugging. "Then there is the money side, I'm not exactly wealthy."

Aimee sat up from her reclining position and looked squarely in the blue eyes. "Then you try again. Have you done any designs?"

"You make it sound so easy. There is so much more involved than just design."

"Of course, there is, Elin. Anything worth doing is involved. You never know until you try."

Elin focused on a distant tree and shrugged. "I have some designs."

"Want to show me?"

A brilliant seductive smile crossed Elin's face. "Do you want to come back to my place and see my etchings?" She wiggled her eyebrows.

Aimee scrambled to her feet and held out her hand. "Let's go…"

The rest of the morning after the show had been one of renewing their deep love and commitment to each other. Elin, standing at the window, watched as a fall rain fell softly on the pavement below. A look of warmth and love crossed her face as she felt the strong, loving arms of Aimee encircle her waist.

"You ready to go?" Aimee asked.

"Yes, we need to get all those flowers over to the hospital today while they are still fresh." She leaned into her lover's body. "Ugh, I need to write thank-you notes." Elin looked into Aimee's green eyes and grimaced. "I hate doing that."

She stole a quick kiss. "Are you sure you want to help me with that? You know you don't have to."

"You know I think we agreed to help each other…do things as a couple." Aimee laughed deeply. "That includes thank-you notes doesn't it?"

"Absolutely. Do you think it is something I need to do myself? You know, the personal touch."

"Perhaps. Tell you what, I'll load the flowers and take them to the hospital and you can get started on the thank-you notes," Aimee offered. "When I get back I can help with the cards or at least put them in the envelopes with stamps.

"Thank you, that will help me." Elin looked at the time. "Come on let's get a move on so we can get it over with. If you'd like, we can go to Frank's for dinner tonight…my treat."

"Sure you don't want to go to some place fancy now that you are 'the new darling of the fashion world'?"

Elin slapped Aimee gently and made a face. "I'm no one's darling but yours."

CHAPTER TWENTY-ONE

Elin sat at her desk with the pile of cards from the flowers in front of her and sighed. *Better get to it.* Her eyes drifted to Aimee who was taking armloads of flowers out to the van. *She has the easier job. Get your rear in gear, Elin, these people thought enough to send congratulatory flowers, the least you can do is thank them.* She picked up the stack and flipped through them looking for the one from her parents. Holding a card in her hand, she shook her head, read it again, then began to shake.

Elin, Congratulations on your success...my money was always on you for greatness. I will be in the audience cheering you on. Love, Marissa.

She dropped all the other cards and gulped in a breath before she whispered, "She was here." A tear coursed its way down her cheek as all the feelings Marissa evoked flooded back.

So much had happened to her since she first met Marissa. She had found love and her true calling in fashion design. Marissa was in the past along with all the old feelings that she invoked. Or is she? Aimee had been her salvation, her lover, and best friend. Yet, just seeing a card that Marissa had written filled her with emotions long buried. She loved Aimee, didn't she? *Of course, I do.* She was everything Elin could have ever hoped for. But then, why did she feel so turned on by this stupid gesture of Marissa?

"I can't let her do this to me, to us. I can't."

Aimee came back inside and looked at her before rushing to her side. "Hey, what's going on? Are you okay?"

Elin, refusing to make eye contact, just handed Aimee the card.

Aimee took the card, read it, and then, breathing deeply, gently placed it on the desk. "Wanna talk about it?"

Elin still wouldn't look at her.

"There's nothing to say. It just took me by surprise that's all." She then gazed into Aimee's eyes and saw the concern there. "Did you get all the flowers loaded?"

"El, I can't believe the nerve of her to send flowers."

"I wasn't expecting it and it just—"

"Damn, you don't need to tell me how you feel, El. Remember I know the feeling and it is like someone punching you in the gut.

"I know."

"The bitch has no heart." Aimee closed her eyes. "I'm sorry I didn't mean the tirade. Why can't she just stay out of our lives?"

"No worries. We have each other and she cannot compete with that."

"I love you. What can I do to help?" Aimee hugged Elin close.

"Since all the flowers are loaded why don't we go deliver them?"

Aimee pointed to the cards and raised an eyebrow. "What about those?"

"I can work on the cards later. Right now I think we need to know that we can do something good for others."

"We can both answer them, Elin." Aimee picked up Marissa's card. "And, hers?" Aimec asked bitterly.

"She doesn't deserve a response." As Aimee turned to leave, Elin picked up Marissa's card and slipped it in her pocket.

†

Aimee eyed Elin as they ate dinner. She knew the look was a result of Marissa entering their lives again. Could they ever get past allowing her to upset their lives? She tried to think of the last time either of them had heard from her. To her best recollection it had been four years ago. Unless Elin hadn't told her otherwise, this was the first contact Elin had with Marissa since that time she met Elin.

"At the risk of sounding like a broken record, do you wanna talk about it?" She was determined to find out why her lover was in such an emotional turmoil. Of course, she knew, but Elin needed to bring it out into the open so they could discuss it together.

"About what?" Elin's eyes concentrated on her plate of linguine.

"You know what, El. Do you remember that we have a deal? We talk about what is going on in our heads regarding *her*." Aimee blew out a breath of frustration and shook her head.

Elin's hand instinctively went to her pocket and she fingered the card. "There's nothing to talk about." She let a small smile to curve her lips. "She's nothing to me, Aimee. Yes, the card upset me but not for the reason you're thinking."

"What am I thinking?"

"That she thinks she still has a hold on me. She doesn't. Not anymore." After placing her fork on the plate, she reached for Aimee's hand. "You are the one that makes my heart smile and sing—no one else does."

"I thought we weren't going to lie to each other about *her*." The visceral reaction Elin had to the card scared Aimee. It was now obvious that Marissa still had a hold of her wife. With her heart breaking, Aimee pulled her hand away and frowned as tears rolled down her cheeks. *Damn it, how can she still get to us after all this time?*

Elin cocked her head and frowned. "I love you and no one else."

"I'm sure you do," Aimee said. The thought of Marissa played on the edges of her mind. "We need to discuss what you're feeling. I love you. You can trust me." They stared at each other.

"I do trust you, Aimee. I feel like I want to run and hide. I don't understand why she called you to come back and never did me. I don't get it."

"Understand? What?"

"Why she called you so many times but not me. Wasn't I good enough?"

"El, this is the first time she's contacted you. You never had the chance to process how you feel and come to terms with something like this."

"But why didn't she call me like she did you?"

"Do you want my best guess?"

Elin nodded.

"Okay here goes. She was your first and you fell for her hard which is exactly what she wanted. What she didn't count on was you pursuing her to the lengths that you did. You stood in the rain waiting for her and I think that spooked her. She couldn't take the chance on it happening again. Calling you for a quickie would only give you hope that she'd be yours. Marissa can't afford that. She's a taker not a giver." Aimee cocked her head. "Does that make sense?"

"She's afraid of me?"

"Basically."

"Then why did she contact me now?"

"Good question that I don't have an answer for. Please let me help you get past this."

"I know how you can do that." The corners of Elin's mouth crinkled in a smile as she reached for Aimee's hand again. "What do you say we go home? I need to feel your arms around me."

Aimee knew that the discussion of Elin's feelings about Marissa and the card were over. She fished in her pocket for money and placed a ten and a twenty on the table. Tonight, they would celebrate their love and push Marissa out of our lives once again. She hoped.

"Let's go."

†

Elin threw a charcoal pencil on the pad in frustration, scraped her chair back, and got up. Concentration was impossible and she knew why. Marissa had invaded her thoughts continually since she read the card from Marissa. She never actually saw the flowers. Someone removed the cards from the flowers with a brief description of what they were on the back. Then Aimee carried them away for the hospital donation.

"Damn, what am I going to do?" She took the card out of her jacket pocket and held it close to her heart. It had been four years since she last spoke to Marissa but the phone number was still etched in her mind. As much as she hated herself for what she was about to do, her fingers, with a mind of their own, quickly punched the buttons.

"Marissa Banks's office. May I help you?" a female's voice asked.

"Yes, this is Elin Prescot. Is there any chance of speaking with Ms. Banks?"

"Just a moment."

Unbelievable! She didn't get the runaround. Fear gripped her heart as she realized that she might just speak with Marissa.

"Elin, is it really you?" Marissa's voice asked happily.

"Um…a…a…yes, it is."

"I am so glad you called. How have you been?"

An edge of happiness to Marissa's tone was something that Elin had never heard before. She couldn't believe that she was hearing the voice she had longed to hear for so many years.

"I...I just wanted to thank you for the flowers they were lovely."

"I'm pleased you like them. Your show was spectacular, Elin. I always knew you were destined for greatness."

The voice sounded so sincere and kind. Who is this person? Had Marissa changed?

"Thank you. I wish I had known you were in the audience. You should have come back stage for the party."

"I didn't think I would be welcomed."

Elin could hear what she thought was hurt in the voice. She was taken aback and she didn't know what to say. Would she have welcomed Marissa? She felt the resounding answer to her question was, "yes."

"It would have been great to see you again, Marissa."

"Have dinner with me."

"I can't."

"Please, I want to see you. I've missed you terribly."

"Did you really? You could have called me...you knew where I lived..."

"You're right, Elin, I thought about you every day. Please see me."

Could it be that Marissa really missed her? She knew how many years it had been. Maybe she had changed maybe...

"No, I can't. I really can't. I'm involved with someone."

"Please," Marissa implored. "Please meet me for dinner. I need to see you."

"When?"

"Friday."

"Where?"

"The Olica. Do you remember it is at the Kimberly? You said it was one of the best meals you ever had."

"What time?"

"Seven."

"I'll be there."

"Thank you, Elin. See you then." Marissa paused. "I love you." The line went dead.

Elin ended the call without a goodbye. She brought her hands to her face and splayed her fingers refusing to let herself have any thoughts of hope where Marissa Banks was concerned.

"What have I done? Oh, Aimee, I am so sorry. What a loser I am."

She pushed aside the guilt over the betrayal to her lover as the vision of Marissa's face drifted into her mind. A warm feeling replaced her self-anger as she recalled the sound of Marissa's voice. Elin wondered if Marissa had really changed much. Was she still as beautiful? Had the last seven years been kind to her?

Aimee's face rose to the surface of her consciousness as the tears that she held in check, rolled down her cheeks. Could she betray Aimee? Hadn't Aimee been there for her, supporting her and loving her? Was she going to allow Marissa who had used them both to come between them? Elin wondered if Aimee would have done the same if the situation were reversed. It didn't take her long to realize that Aimee would never betray her with the likes of Marissa Banks.

"I need to get out of here and visit my favorite place." The viewing deck at the Empire State Building. Elin blew out a disgusted breath furious with herself.

For the next two days, guilt and shame filled Elin. At the same time, the anticipation of seeing Marissa again turned her on as nothing had since she had last been with her. Nights would find her in Aimee's arms making love with a ferocity that they had never experienced. They didn't speak during the evenings, each lost in their own thoughts.

CHAPTER TWENTY-TWO

Ever since the fashion show, Aimee would stare at her with a questioning look and Elin would always look away. While at the hospital, waiting for a patient's x-rays, Aimee realized that their relationship had changed, and she knew why: Marissa Banks. How could she fault Elin when she had felt the same overwhelming influence on more occasions than she cared to remember? How would she react if Marissa called her? Her mind drifted back two years when her cell phone rang and how overwhelmed she had felt when she heard Marissa's voice…

"Aimee, I need to see you tomorrow night," the authoritative voice said. "You know where to meet me."

"A hello would have been nice." She blew out a breath.

"Just be there."

"No can do, Marissa."

"Unacceptable."

"Maybe so, but I won't be there. How many times do I have to tell you that before you will believe me? I've moved on and it doesn't include you," Aimee said.

"I haven't time to play this game, Aimee. I will expect you at seven."

The phone went dead, and Aimee just stared at it.

"The nerve of her. Wait until I tell Elin." Her mind fought with her body as the old familiar feelings of the lust Marissa caused tried to take hold. "Maybe I won't tell her." The next night, Aimee told Elin she had to work late and went to the special meeting place and clandestinely watched as Marissa waited for her. Aimee watched Marissa sitting there and for the first time felt that she had the power. She could choose to go to Marissa or leave. She left…

Now, a patient was keeping Aimee at the hospital when all she wanted to do was go home and tell Elin about that remembered incident. Elin was having a hard time and she knew if she shared her experience, she could help her. When she heard her lover's voice on her cell phone she smiled.

"Hey, I've got a critical patient, so don't wait dinner. I'm not sure when I'll be home."

"Do what you need to, Aims, I will be here when you get home."

"Thanks. Hey, when I get home, I have something important to tell you," she said before adding, "Elin?"

"Yes."

"I love you so much. Thank you for being there for me."

"Anytime. Hurry home."

Elin sat down at the table and ate a lonely meal…looking around the home that she and Aimee shared, wondering what it would be like not to have her wife and lover in her life. Did she really love Aimee or was she just a substitute for Marissa because of shared experiences? A shiver shot through her body as she recalled the unbridled passion she had felt for Marissa. Putting the food away and the dishes in the dishwasher, she headed for the shower and bed. All the while thoughts of Marissa danced through her mind.

A few hours later, Aimee crawled in next to her and kissed her cheek.

"You are home," a sleepy Elin said.

"Yeah, it's late, go back to sleep."

"How's your patient?"

"He's going to make it."

"I'm glad. What did you want to tell me?" Elin asked as she drifted back to sleep.

"It'll wait until morning."

"Okay." Elin snuggled closer and her breathing soon evened out.

Elin entered the house and went up a staircase before she noticed that the walls, ceilings, and floors were all gone, and the steps were only one thin board wide. Reaching the landing, she saw the rafters that supported the non-existent floor. Across the way was a door with a familiar figure standing in it.

Terrified yet comforted by the sight, she asked, "Who are you?"

The figure began hovering just above the rafters with a long white finger beckoning her. "Come to me," a haunting voice called.

She tried desperately to see who it was but a white fog was clouding the face. She felt unconditional love from the entity and knew it could only be Aimee. A sense of warmth filled her heart.

Looking at the spindly rafters, she shook her head. "I can't it won't support me."

The figure, floating back toward the door, drifted inside.

"Don't go, please wait for me. I'll find a way."

"It's too late for that. You betrayed me."

A great sense of loss filled her subconscious as her body trembled. Turning, she saw a menacing figure, encased in flames, moving up the stairway toward her. Fear filled her heart as the apparition began to engulf her in a fiery embrace while seductively touching her skin. She felt something piercing her as if someone was devouring her flesh down to the bone.

Desperate to get away, her arms raised, and her clenched fists began beating back the flames as her eyes tried to see the face.

"No," she screamed as she recognized who was trying to consume her greedily—Marissa wouldn't let her go.

"It's okay it's only a dream." Aimee wrapped her arms around the flailing Elin and pulled her into a loving embrace.

Elin's eyes flew open. "Oh, Aimee, I am so sorry."

"Hey, nothing to be sorry for. I wasn't asleep."

"No," Elin said shakily. "Not for that." Lifting her head, her teary eyes searched out Aimee the one she did love. "I called her...I told her I would meet her for dinner tomorrow night. Why did I do that? Why?"

Aimee kissed the top of the dark hair and held her lover closer. Elin's confession didn't surprise her. When she had seen the card, she had known exactly what Elin's reaction would be. After all, she had the same feelings two years earlier when Marissa called her out of the blue.

"What do you say we put an end to this for once and all?"

"You're leaving me?" Elin pulled back.

Surprised by the comment, Aimee frowned. "Never. I meant let's put an end to Marissa in our lives. We can't move forward if she is lurking in every corner."

"How do we do that? All she had to do was send some flowers with a stupid card and I am slinking around, trying to see her again."

A sly smile crossed Aimee's face. "I have a plan...are you in?"

"Yes."

†

A nervous Elin walked into the restaurant and rubbed the nape of her neck nervously, experiencing the pull of Marissa long before she saw her. Light blue eyes found her, searing her with desire and passion. Feet moving of their own accord, found their way to the table where she clung to the chair back for support. Her knees threatened to give out. Marissa was at her side wrapping an arm around her for support.

"Are you okay?" she asked gently.

"Thank you." The closeness of Marissa made Elin feel lightheaded as she allowed Marissa to guide her into the chair. She looked curiously at Marissa. Something was different about her. She was being gentle and kind which was something she didn't equate with the woman. Was it possible that Marissa had changed?

"Certainly," Marissa replied as she took her own seat. Smoldering eyes appraised her. "You are looking well."

"Thank you." Elin briefly closed her eyes then smiled back at Marissa.

"You're show was outstanding. When you came out and took your bow, I thought that success looked good on you."

"Had I known you were there, Marissa, I would have invited you to come backstage and join the party."

"Believe me I wanted to." She smiled seductively. "You and I have this...um, connection and... well, let's just say it wouldn't have done for the star to disappear."

Elin gulped down the urge to let her stomach purge itself and smiled. "Yes, it wouldn't have been a good idea."

A young, attractive waitress approached the table. Her face was flushed, and her eyes raked over Marissa. "Ms. Banks, would you care for something from the bar?" she asked with a flirty tone.

Marissa's eyes never left the ample breast.

"Yes." Marissa's hand reached out and touched the girl's arm. "We will have the house Merlot." Her eyes moved up to capture the brown ones as her hand moved back to the table. "Thank you, Kait."

Marissa turned back to Elin and smiled. "I remember how fond you were of the Merlot the last time we ate here."

She hadn't changed at all. Elin couldn't believe she ever entertained the idea of being with her again. As she watched Marissa seducing the young waitress, Elin's stomach churned. *Back off bitch, tonight she's mine, you can have her later.*

Kait returned to the table with the drinks. "Would you like to order now?"

Again, Marissa's eyes captured the young waitress and she said, "Hmm, Elin, is there anything you'd like to eat?"

Elin couldn't believe the sexual comment Marissa made while looking at the young girl. Had neither of them any pride? It was overtly obvious that Marissa hadn't changed and never would. The waitress was grinning at her with unabashed lust.

"I'll let you select what and where we eat, Marissa," Elin said.

Marissa looked away from the girl and nodded before she stood. "Charge the drinks to my room and be sure to give yourself a generous tip." Then she leaned into the waitress, whispered something that made the young woman smile and gently kissed her cheek. Taking a few steps, she stood by Elin.

"Shall we go? I'm very hungry."

Elin held the anger rising to the surface. How dare Marissa treat her so callously. She needed to get her emotions in check. She was there to put Marissa out of her life and needed all the strength of character she could muster.

They stood hip to hip in the elevator that they shared with two other couples. Marissa's hand, finding its way to her back, gently rubbed her waistline. Elin could feel her heart racing when they exited the elevator. Her anticipation grew as her steps took her closer to Marissa's suite. Her goal was in reach.

Marissa swiped her keycard and opened the door. "Here we are. I hope you're as hungry as I am."

"Mmm-hmm," Elin said as she entered the room. "All my dreams are about to come true." She turned and smiled seductively as Marissa began to close the door only to have it pushed back open.

"What are you doing here?" Marissa demanded.

"Oh, I came to watch." Aimee shoved her way into the room.

"No one invited you. Now get out," Marissa demanded.

Aimee walked over to Elin, pulled her close, and kissed her soundly. "Oh, I was invited. Wasn't I, darling?"

"Yes." Elin kissed her wife again.

With eyes wide and mouth opened, Marissa was specchless—something that was foreign to her. Here, in her domain, she called all the shots and no one else. She wouldn't allow it. She had to regain her equilibrium and not let the two women make a mockery out of her.

"Hmm, it has been a long time since I had two beautiful women in my bed at the same time." She moved closer and gave the couple a lustful look. "Oh, yes, the two of you pleasuring me at the same time will be spectacular."

Aimee was the first to speak. "I don't think you understand, Marissa. You aren't part of this equation."

Marissa's face filled with rage. "Excuse me? You have no say in this. Elin is here to be with me."

"No, I'm not. I'm here with my wife to get you out of our lives."

Veins popped out on the long neck as fury gained a foothold. "I'll never be out of your life." She pointed toward Aimee. "You want her over me? Get real. She isn't even a good fuck."

"Now, that is where you are wrong. Aimee is everything I ever want."

"Did she ever tell you how she drugged you then laid down on your couch with me and screamed out my name for more? Or how we did it for hours while you were under the influence of the sedative, she gave you? She couldn't get enough." A cruel laugh emanated from Marissa. Seeing the wounded look in Elin's eyes, she knew she had hit the mark.

Aimee put a protective arm around Elin's shoulder.

"I was her first, Aimee, and you will never measure up. Does she still taste wonderful or did she just produce that special elixir for me?" Maliciously she added, "Do her fingers do that special move inside you? I had her first and taught her everything. No wonder you want her…it's like having me all the time." She grasped Elin's arm and pulled her close. "Let's go. I've wasted too much time on this charade."

Elin wrestled her arm away. "You are so egotistical! Don't you get it? I don't want anything to do with you. I'm nothing more than another conquest to you. Go fuck that waitress. No, on second thought don't, she deserves so much better." Elin took Aimee's hand. "Come on let's go, we're finished here."

"No one leaves me," Marissa shrieked as they opened the door.

"Get used to it, Marissa. You're not getting any younger. Sooner rather than later, no one will want you unless you pay them," Elin spat out angrily. "Maybe you should get yourself a cat if you want a pussy."

"Please don't leave," Marissa whispered. "I need you."

Elin refused to let the pull ensnare her and shook her head. She knew that there was no way Marissa was going to let Elin leave until she got what she wanted. Elin in her bed.

"Well, I don't need you anymore." She walked through the door and closed it gently.

CHAPTER TWENTY-THREE

Elin and Aimee stood close together holding hands and smiling broadly as they rode the elevator.

"We did it!"

"We did indeed. I feel so free." Elin sighed in deep satisfaction. She thought for a moment. "Did you see how hard she squeezed her eyes to get the tears to fall? I actually felt sorry for her."

"I didn't," Aimee growled. "Don't waste your time feeling sorry for her it was just another of her tactics to get you to stay."

"I know, but there was something different about her this time. She almost begged me to stay," Elin said.

"Yeah, she isn't getting any younger, so conquests aren't as available." The elevator door opened. "Wait for me outside and I'll bring the car around."

Elin hadn't noticed the young waitress standing outside the hotel entrance until the girl spoke.

"Wow, I can't believe she is done with you so soon," an amused voice said.

Elin tilted her head. "What do you mean?"

"She usually keeps them overnight."

"You should be careful around her, she's a user."

"Duh, well yeah. I've seen her here with so many women that it doesn't take a rocket scientist to figure that one out." Kait laughed.

"You're on to her?"

"Hey, she is a great tipper, available whenever I need a bed partner and...well you know...she's really a stud."

Elin frowned then laughed. "You're using her?"

"Why else would I waste my time on an old broad like her? Besides, there are always hundreds of other fish in the sea and some of them end up in this hotel."

Startled, all Elin could think was, *another Marissa in the making.* She let out a small laugh. *Exactly what she deserves.*

†

Elin and Aimee sat close on their couch at home and held each other tight. The events earlier had eradicated Marissa Banks from their lives for good. Elin told Aimee what the waitress told her about Marissa.

"You should have seen her in the restaurant, chatting up the waitress while I was sitting there. I think she wanted to make me jealous or something. Shame she didn't hear what the waitress told me later." Elin giggled, and squeezed Aimee's hand. "All I could think was that tonight was mine with Marissa. The girl would get hers but only get a few days." She chuckled. "Now it would seem it is Marissa's turn to be played. That girl is Marissa only twenty years younger."

"It sounds like she's finally getting what she deserves. She's met her match and I can't think of anyone who deserves it more." Aimee laughed a moment before the laughter stopped. Indignation laced Aimee's voice. "Can you imagine she actually thought she was going to have a threesome?"

"Arrogance—she has that about her, we both know that. I guess that is why she can con so many into her bed. We were classic examples."

"Perhaps."

"For a moment there tonight, I actually thought she had changed, and she really did care."

"What if she had, what would you do then?" Aimee asked, afraid of what Elin might say.

"She hasn't changed and even if she did, you are the one that I love, not her. Besides, when she went after the waitress, I knew it was all an act. She comes across as sincere and charming but she's not. Why? What makes her do this to people?"

Aimee hugged Elin closer. "Because she can. She has nothing to lose really. She doesn't let her heart rule her carnal desires, therefore she offers nothing but a good fuck."

"Hmm, she was that," Elin said pensively. "But love is so much more than just mind-blowing sex. Why did we allow ourselves to think there was a chance?"

"She played on our insecurities. There she was, bigger than life. A gorgeous woman who oozed sensuality, power, and confidence, and she wanted you. What a trip it is to think someone like her wanted you." Shaking her head, Aimee let out a small laugh. "Every time she'd call, I would think, this is the time, this is the moment when she will stay with me forever. I think it eventually became a challenge for me to see if I could ever be good enough for her."

"You are better than her. You know how to love."

Kissing Elin's cheek, Aimee embraced her, then let go.

"Just a minute, I want to show you something." Getting up, she went to the closet, pulled out a shoebox, and came back to the couch.

"Whatcha got there?"

Aimee lifted the lid and dumped out all the contents. "This is my Marissa collection. It represents all the times we spent together." She picked up a book of matches. "This is our first date." Moving the items around, she grabbed a napkin. "And this is from a bar where she met me six months after she dumped me."

Elin held up a hand and said, "Just a minute."

She got up and went into the bedroom. Coming back out, she too had an old shoebox. "Here is my collection."

Aimee's eyes widened as Elin's *treasures* joined hers. "Oh, my God, we are such goofs. I can't believe we did this!"

"Do you think all her conquests have a box too?" Elin giggled. "We really are pathetic." Picking up a matchbook, Elin's eyes twinkled. "What do you say we end this once and for all?"

"Sounds good to me."

They gathered everything except two matchbooks and tossed it all into the fireplace before placing a few logs on top of the pile. They both tore off a match and struck it.

"On the count of three. One, two three."

With great happiness laced with a sense of release, they set fire to all that was Marissa Banks. They had finally eradicated her hold on their lives, allowing their love to flourish unabated.

"We finally did it. Can you believe it?" Elin asked as she leaned into Aimee. "I feel lighter somehow."

"Together," Aimee whispered. "Do you see that those memories have burned, igniting a new flame. Our flame. I love you, Elin. All of you, now and forever."

"As I love you, Aims." She laid down on the carpet in front of the fire and held out a hand.

Aimee knelt down and kissed her wife. At first, their kisses were tentative, but it wasn't long before lips feverishly began exploring with purpose. Soon they were naked, pledging their undying love for each other. Their memories of Marissa, long burned, were gone forever. In its place was an unquenchable fire for each other that would last a lifetime.

ABOUT THE AUTHOR

ERIN O'REILLY

Erin O'Reilly is an accomplished author with twenty-three published works, including her newest collaborations with JM Dragon: 'Please Don't Go'. Her focus as a writer is to develop strong characters that make a dramatic impact on her storylines.

When not writing, she is the Technical Director and CEO of Affinity Rainbow Publications.

Contact Erin at:
erinoreilly55@gmail.com

OTHER AFFINITY BOOKS

<u>At Last</u> by JM Dragon
A perfume company in trouble, leading to a town in peril.
Old Loves. Unrequited Loves. New passions. Can the
reclusive Gene Desrosiers save her family company and the
people she cares for, even though some are not aware of it
yet? Will an ultimate sacrifice win the day, or will Grady end
up a ghost town of unfulfilled lives? This love story will
warm your heart.

<u>Deuce</u> by Jen Silver
When Jay Reid was in her twenties, she had it all. A
professional tennis career, Charlotte, the love of her life and
a new baby. Charlotte's research vessel, *RV Caspian*, was
lost at sea, leaving Jay to raise their child alone. Rescued by
a local fisherman, with no memory of her life before, she
lives on the Faroe Islands as Katrin Nielsen. Seeing a
beached seal one day triggers her memory. Twenty-three
years is a long time. Is the love they once shared strong

enough to be rekindled or have too many years passed eroding all hope of a happy ever after?

After Dark by Samantha Hicks
Can a love that starts out in terror be real or last? Meredith Ashcroft disappears on her way to a client meeting. Five months later, art gallery manager Stephanie Edwards is also held and tortured by the same sadistic man. Thrown together trying to overcome their shared ordeal, they find themselves falling in love. Is it true love or just an attachment to each other born out of fear for their lives?

The Book Witch by Annette Mori
What if someone had the power to bring characters from a book to life...should they be allowed to glimpse reality? Imara is that person, a book witch who is convinced of her superiority, especially over book magicians. Join award-winning author, Annette Mori, and the gang from Asset Management, The Organization, and the colorful women in The Book Addict to bring you this delightful, magical romance.

Calling Home by Jen Silver
Sarah Frost enjoys her dream job as director of the Frost Foundation making her home at one of their writers' retreats, The Lodge on the Lake. Galen Thomas, taking an extended break from her vet's practice arrives at the island to fill the post of handy person. The island idyll is soon undermined by the revelation of events from forty years earlier, threatening the lives and loves of Sarah, Berry, and Galen. Calling home

and what they now call home—all are affected by the disturbing legacy from the past.

Reach of the Heron by Angela Koenig
After an automobile accident takes the lives of her parents and nearly her own, Arkadia O'Malley faces a painful recovery. As she seeks custody of her younger sister, Rini, she must also contend with the obstruction of Irish law. When Rini is moved from a harsh orphanage to one of the notoriously cruel Magdalene homes, Arkadia's efforts to reunite with her sister are aided by powerful women from this reality as well as from Elsewhere.

From Wind and Water by Laura Kovack
The Seventh Kingdom is surrounded by the Lands of Earth, Fire, Water and Wind. All but Earth have rulers. When a new enemy threatens all of the Lands, it is imperative to find the last ruler of Earth. Morgayne, ruler in Land of Water and Ventus, ruler of Land of Wind, form a tentative yet skeptical relationship—everything depends on them. Will that tie survive the battles ahead? Will they allow or deny their feelings in this fantasy adventure that will have you urging them on to victory on all fronts.

The Book Addict by Annette Mori
From award-winning author Annette Mori comes the captivating story of Tanya, a young woman whose life is unremarkable without any friends or lovers. Then she meets Elle, the alluring owner of the new bookstore, The Enchanted Page. Elle looks like she stepped out of a Nordic adventure and Tanya is immediately infatuated with the mysterious woman. Join the colorful characters as they try to right the

wrongs created by Elle's fiercest foe. And just maybe, the books won't be the only thing enchanted if Elle allows the magic of love to enter her heart.

Colors of Rage by Nanisi Barrett D'Arnuk
Dr. Kailyn DeKendran, head of the Acoustic Research Department, and her sister Jayanta, are drawn into the fray of unrest during the election season when the participants can't remember why they are rioting. When Kailyn disappears, family and friends band together to find her. Time is running out, and the riots are getting more violent. Will they find Kailyn before it is too late to put an end to the madness that has overtaken them?

Naomi's Soul by Renee MacKenzie
This second book in the Karst Series picks up the Peace Movement where Kai's Heart left off. Everyone is still struggling to find the balance between reconciliation and guarding. Control must remain in the hands of those working diligently for peace in the war and disease ravaged New America. Warrior Naomi Adams is on a routine mission for the Peace Movement when tragedy strikes her contingent. She will need to dig deep to find the strength to move past the devastating earthquake that has split up her party.

My Starlight by Loryn Stone
If only we could have met sooner...
Orly Kochav likes nerdy things. A huge fan of Japanese animation, cosplay, and playing the bass, she's convinced she can use her natural charisma and swagger to get anything she wants. Including beautiful girls. When her judgmental mother catches her kissing a girl and asks her a hideous

question, Orly goes into a state of emotional hiding. Now sixteen, Orly is itching to reclaim her prior life and when a new friend informs her that a secret club dedicated to their favorite Japanese Anime, Lovely Starlight Fighter, is at their high school, Orly thinks she'll be able to slip back into the world of fandom without issue. Until she meets the club's vice president, Danielle Cohen and the rising attraction to her threatens to make Orly question every choice she's about to make.

True North by Ali Spooner
Cam's story continues as the Gator Girlz business continues to thrive under her leadership, but will self-doubt jeopardize her relationship when Bugsy reveals the family moonshine business to an unsuspecting Luce? Will a devastating injury to Sandy end her career as a gator hunter or will it open a door to love? Join the St. Angelo family for a third adventure to find out more about life, loving, and family in Bayou Country.

The Dream Catcher by Annette Mori
What if all your dreams—the good ones and the nightmares—came to life in the real world?
Heaven is a Dream Weaver, and that is her reality. When she wakes up, she never knows what will greet her or her best friend and roommate, Syl. It could be a sexy stripper or a monster from another dimension. When Syl suggests a Dream Catcher to help her control the dreams, Heaven is wary until she meets the alluring Maya. Between the government and the powerful Dream Catching sisters, time is running out for Heaven. She wonders who she can trust. Can

this lovely Dream Catcher protect her or is Heaven truly on her own?

Gator Girlz by Ali Spooner
In the sequel to Diamond Dreams, Cam St. Angelo finished her freshman year on a high. Her softball career is on path. Everything seems to fall in place for Cam and Tab as the new school year and softball season take off. All too soon, unfortunate events at the home front force Cam to leave college and her softball dreams behind. As always, it's family first.

The Tempest by JM Dragon
Doctor Alana Cameron has dedicated her life to working on the family legacy, a transportation device which will change the world for everyone, called Tempest. Tragedy has dogged the project over the years, causing military intervention. Super soldier Major Denise Tranter, who loyally defends Earth in any way possible, finds herself drawn into the Tempest program. Emotional bonding is not in her remit, although she finds herself inexplicably drawn to Alana.

Trusting Hearts by Samantha Hicks
When successful advertising executive Carrie-Ann Stedman is tasked to train a new hire, she is reluctant. She has never forgiven Holly Fletcher, the newbie, for stealing an important client away from her. Holly doesn't know what Carrie's problem with her is. When the two are thrown together, can they build a working relationship without business getting in the way of the growing attraction between them?

Free to Love by Ali Spooner and Annette Mori
Captain Hillary Blythe loves sailing the ocean. Her journeys along the Atlantic Coast and Caribbean to deliver goods contain many adventures. When she brings a small group of rescued Africans to the Methodist mission on Antigua, challenges to deeply ingrained beliefs arise when devoted Christian, Elizabeth Allen, is drawn to one of the women, Kia. Will Kia and Elizabeth be free to love among the harsh laws of the land and Elizabeth's struggles with her faith?

Kai's Heart by Renee MacKenzie
The time has come for the Resistance to take back control of New America from the Anointed tyrants. Growing up as the daughter of a Resistance Army General, Kai Brodie's focus is keenly on the upcoming Revolution. So how is it then that she can't take her eyes off the beautiful Anointed guard? Can Kai break free from tradition and find love in the arms of someone her upbringing tells her she should hate? Can she protect her love from those who hunt them? Will Kai and Rachel survive the battle over the fate of their beloved New America?

Diamond Dreams by Ali Spooner
Cameron St. Angelo dreams of playing softball in the College World Series. Earning a scholarship to play ball for her beloved LSU brings Cam one step closer to achieving this dream. When Cam arrives on campus, she joins a family of women who share her love of the sport, and she realizes there is room in her life for another love.

Affinity
Rainbow Publications

eBooks, Print, Free eBooks

Visit our website for more publications available online.

www.affinityrainbowpublications.com

Published by Affinity Rainbow Publications
A Division of Affinity eBook Press NZ LTD
Canterbury, New Zealand

Registered Company 2517228

www.ingramcontent.com/pod-product-compliance
Lightning Source LLC
Chambersburg PA
CBHW052031020726
47501CB00004B/1358